1999

101 WAYS TO MAKE EVERY SECOND COUNT

Time management tips and techniques for more success with less stress

101 WAYS TO MAKE EVERY SECOND COUNT

Time management tips and techniques for more success with less stress

By
Robert W. Bly

CAREER PRESS

Franklin Lakes, NJ

101 WAYS TO MAKE EVERY SECOND COUNT
Cover design by Barry Littmann
Printed in the U.S.A. by Book-mart Press

To order this title, please call toll-free 1-800-CAREER-1 (NJ and Canada: 201-848-0310) to order using VISA or Master-Card, or for further information on books from Career Press.

The Career Press, Inc., 3 Tice Road, PO Box 687, Franklin Lakes, NJ 07417

Library of Congress Cataloging-in-Publication Data

Bly, Robert W.
    101 ways to make every second count : time management tips and techniques for more success with less stress / by Robert W. Bly.
        p.   cm.
    Includes index.
    ISBN 1-56414-406-2 (pbk.)
    1. Time management.   I. Title.   II. Title: One hundred one ways to make every second count.   III. Title: One hundred and one ways to make every second count.
HD69.T4B57   1999
650.1—dc21   99-25026
                                                                        CIP

Dedication

To Eleanor Brangan, who taught me how to write

Acknowledgments

Thanks to the staff at Career Press for having faith in me and in this book...and then helping me to make the manuscript much better than it was when it first crossed their desks.

Contents

Introduction

"You may delay, but Time will not."
—Benjamin Franklin, American statesman and philosopher

I'm looking at my watch. It's 8:38 on a Friday morning. By my calculations, I have only approximately 204,400 waking hours of life left. And I intend to make the most of the time still available to me. How about you?

Today, the demands on our time are tremendous. Everyone has too much to do and not enough time to do it. According to an article in *Men's Health* magazine (March, 1997), 42 percent of American workers believe they are overloaded with work.

We live in the Age of Now. Customers are more demanding than ever. They want everything yesterday. As *Miami Herald* columnist Leonard Pitts comments, "We move faster than ever, but never quite fast enough." (*The Record*, October 27, 1997)

"When our society travels at electronic speed, we fall under the sway of a new force...the power of *now*," says Stephen Bertman, a professor at the University of Windsor, in the article

"Stephen Bertman on Hyperculture." (*Future Times,* Fall, 1998). "It replaces duration with immediacy, permanence with transcience, memory with sensation, insight with impulse." He argues that this acceleration of change contributes to "a growing sense of stress, disorientation, and loss." On the other hand, if you master strategies for coping with today's accelerated pace, you can meet the demands placed upon you while still having time for yourself.

According to an article in *American Demographics* (January, 1999), consumers have come to view time as their most precious commodity: "To satisfy today's consumer, you need to do business in a real-time world—one in which time and distance collapse, action and response are simultaneous, and customers demand instant gratification."

"We've learned to live by the Rule of 6," notes Gary Springer in an article in the *Business-to-Business Marketer* (February, 1998). "What used to take six months, now takes six weeks; what used to take six weeks now is wanted in six days; what normally took six days is needed in six hours; and what used to be done in six hours is now expected in six minutes." Technology, says Springer, is responsible for much of this change.

Downsizing has left organizations leaner and meaner. Thousands of workers have been fired, and those who remain must take up the slack and are working harder than ever. According to a Harris poll, the average work week increased from 41 to 50 hours between 1973 and 1993.

A radio commercial for Bigelow Herbal Tea observes, "We seem to live our lives in perpetual motion." In fact, we're so busy, we don't even have time to eat! For instance, the "lunch hour" is disappearing from the American business world. Workers more frequently eat lunch at their desks. The article "Shrinking Lunch Hours" (*The Futurist*, August/September, 1998) tells us that 40 percent take no lunch break at all and the typical lunch break is 36 minutes, although many people use that time to take care of personal business rather than eat. Recently I read that cereal sales are declining because cereal and milk can't be eaten in the car while driving; breakfast bars meet that need better.

In her book *The Worst Years of Our Lives* (HarperPerennial), Barbara Ehrenreich writes:

> I don't know when the cult of conspicuous busyness began, but it has swept up almost all the upwardly mobile, professional women I know. Already, it is getting hard to recall the days when, for example, "Let's have lunch," meant something other than, "I've got more important things to do than talk to you right now." There was even a time when people used to get together without the excuse of needing to eat something—when, in fact, it was considered rude to talk with your mouth full. In the old days, hardly anybody had an appointment book...
>
> It's not only women, of course; for both sexes, busyness has become an important insignia of upper-middle-class status. Nobody, these days, admits to having a hobby, although two or more careers—say, neurosurgery and an art dealership—is not uncommon, and I am sure we will soon be hearing more about the tribulations of the four-paycheck couple...

You can't jam 25 hours into a 24-hour day. Time is a non-renewable resource that's consumed at a constant and relentless rate. Once an hour is gone, it's gone forever; you can never get it back.

Yet you can solve most of your time-related problems—not enough time, too much to do, deadlines too short, bosses too demanding, not getting to your own priorities—simply by increasing the productivity of the one resource you *can* control: you. As management consultant Stephen Covey notes "The only person over whom you have direct and immediate control is yourself."

Some human resource professionals refer to the people in their organizations as "resources." That's cold, but in a way, appropriate and accurate. You are a resource. You have output. To succeed today, you need to increase your output to the next level without making the resource sick, tired, dissatisfied, or unhappy. That's where this book can help.

101 Ways to Make Every Second Count shows you how to succeed in today's competitive, fast-paced world by increasing your own personal productivity, so you can get more done in less time. Going beyond conventional time management, *101 Ways to Make Every Second Count* offers diverse strategies and tactics in order to empower you to gain this productivity boost—everything from planning, scheduling, organizing, and eliminating time-wasters, to suggestions on improving life habits that give you more energy so you can work better and faster, to using the latest technology to manage information and communicate more efficiently and effectively.

After reading this book you will be better equipped to:

🕐 Get more done in less time.

🕐 Meet deadlines and commitments.

🕐 Have time left over for the things you really *want* to do.

🕐 Increase customer satisfaction.

🕐 Enhance your on-the-job performance.

🕐 Have more time for family, personal, and other important activities.

🕐 Feel better and have more energy.

🕐 Eliminate time-wasters.

🕐 Benefit from the latest time-saving technologies.

🕐 Improve your efficiency.

🕐 Find the information you need easier and faster.

🕐 Reduce pressure and stress.

🕐 Get through your work backlog.

101 Ways to Make Every Second Count is organized into 10 quick-reading chapters. The first chapter presents proven time-saving strategies you can learn in less than 20 minutes to achieve an instant boost in personal productivity. Chapter 2 enables you to assess how important increasing personal productivity is to you...and whether you are willing to do what is necessary to achieve it. Chapters 3 through 10 present a wealth of tactics that can help you get more done in less time with less stress—with no sacrifice in the quality of the work.

The English author Samuel Butler called time "the only true purgatory," and Ralph Waldo Emerson said time is "the surest poison." But I disagree. How you use your time is largely up to you. *101 Ways to Make Every Second Count* shows you how to transform time from an enemy into an ally—and become the master of your time, rather than its slave. The best time to start? Right now.

I do have one favor to ask. If you have a personal productivity technique that works for you, why not send it to me so I can share it with readers of the next edition of this book? You will receive full credit, of course. Contact me at the following address:

Bob Bly
Center for Technical Communication
22 E. Quackenbush Avenue
Dumont, NJ 07628
Phone: 201-385-1220
Fax: 201-385-1138
E-mail: rwbly@bly.com
Web: www.bly.com

And now, let's get started!

Chapter 1

Work Habits That Speed You Up

"I am always quarreling with time! It is so short to do something and so long to do nothing."
—Queen Charlotte, Heir to the British throne 1796-1817

The ability to work faster and get more done in less time isn't slavery; it's freedom. You're going to have the same big pile of stuff to do every day whether you want it or not. If you can be more efficient, you can get it done and still have some time left over for yourself—whether it's to read the paper, play with your kids, jog, or play the piano.

Make to-do lists

Productive workers have schedules and stick with them. But according to an article in *The Competitive Advantage* (February, 1996), more than 50 percent of workers don't schedule their daily activities.

It's not enough to know the projects you're working on. You should break your day into segments. I suggest using hour increments, although quarter and half days can also work. Write down on a piece of paper the project you will work on during each of those segments.

Do this every day, at the beginning of your workday (or, if you prefer, do it the last thing in the day to prepare for the next day). Post your hour-by-hour schedule for the day on a wall or a corkboard by your desk so it is always in view.

Although I may work on a particular project for more than one hour a day, these hours need not be scheduled consecutively. It's up to you.

As you go through the day, consult your schedule to keep on track. If priorities change, you can change the schedule, but do this in writing. Revise and post the schedule. Keeping your schedule on your computer makes this a simple task you can do in minutes.

Why do hour increments work so well? Precisely because they give you a deadline—one hour—to get things done. "Work expands so as to fill time available for its completion," writes C. Noarthcote Parkinson in his book *Parkinson's Law* (Houghton Mifflin). If you have all day to do task X, you'll take all day. If you have only an hour, you'll work that much more quickly and efficiently.

It's okay to redo the schedule as long as you don't miss deadlines. Some days I redo the daily to-do schedule two or three times, depending on deadlines and inspiration. Why not? As long as you are organized, keep track of deadlines, and allow enough time to finish each job, you will increase your productivity by working on things you feel in the mood to work on.

The 3 to-do lists you should keep

The key component of my personal productivity system is a series of lists I keep on my computer. In fact, I have so many lists, that I have a file called "Lists" to keep track of them! That way, I make sure the set of lists I review each day covers every one of my tasks.

Making lists is a simple idea, but extremely effective. Some people credit Ivy Lee, one of the first management consultants, for first using lists as a formal time-management system.

As the story goes, Charles Schwab, president of Bethlehem Steel in the early 1900s, couldn't seem to get enough done. Details and minor matters were crowding the time he urgently needed to consider more important matters. He asked Ivy Lee what to do about it.

Lee handed Schwab a blank sheet of paper. "Write down," he said, "the most important things you have to do tomorrow. The first thing tomorrow morning, start working on item number one, and stay with it until completed. Then take item number two the same way. Then number three, and so on. Don't worry if you don't complete everything on the schedule. At least you will have accomplished the most important projects before getting to the less important ones."

The steel executive tried the idea and recommended it to his associates because the method worked so well. When Schwab asked Lee what his fee was, Lee replied "Pay me what you think the idea is worth." Schwab reportedly sent Lee a check for $25,000—a fortune in those days (*Time Management: The Art of Getting Things Done,* Economics Press, 1971).

"If you are thinking that lists can be confining, you'll soon learn that once you get used to using them, you'll find them liberating," writes Dan Kennedy in his book *No B.S. Time Management for Entrepreneurs* (Self Counsel Press). "The more details you get on paper, the fewer you must remember and worry about. This frees your mind up for more important tasks."

Every morning, I come into the office and turn on my computer. After checking my various online services for e-mail, I open the LIST file; it tells me which lists I must read and review to start my day.

The most important lists on my LIST file are my to-do lists. I keep several, but the most critical are my daily to-do list, projects to-do list, and long-term to-do list:

1. *Daily to-do list.* Each day I type up and post a list of the items I have to do that day. From this list, I create my hour-by-hour schedule. This list is revised daily. I enjoy work and put in long hours, so I take on a lot of projects that interest me. But I never take on more than I can handle, so I can continue to meet all deadlines.

2. *Projects to-do list.* In a separate computer file, I keep a list of all of my projects currently under contract, along with the deadline for each. I review this list several times a week, using it to make sure the daily to-do list covers all essential items that have to be done right away.

3. *Long-term to-do list.* This is a list of projects I want to do at some point, but are not now under contract and therefore do not have any assigned deadlines. I check this list about once a week, and usually put in a few hours each week on a few of the projects from this list that interest me most.

This simple system works. Most of the techniques throughout this book are simple, yet powerful, so don't be put off by their brevity or ease of implementation. I agree with Texaco CEO Peter Bijur, who said, "As soon as you start to introduce complexity, whether it's into an organization or a set of responsibilities, the more difficult it is to operate." I also agree with Hair Club for Men CEO Sy Sperling: "Simple solutions are the best solutions."

> "Lists work only if they are 100-percent leakproof," notes personal productivity coach David Allen in an interview with *Fast Company* magazine (May, 1998). For instance, if your "to-call" list doesn't include all of the phone calls you have to make, then your mind still has to remember some of them.

Determine priorities

Can you *always* work on what you want to work on, right when you want to work on it? No. Sometimes, a pressing deadline means putting aside a more pleasurable task to do something more formidable—even if you don't feel like doing it immediately.

On the wall of my office near my desk, I have posted a list that I update every week. It's called, "Rules of the Office," and it reminds me of what I have to do to be successful in my business. Rule #1 is "First things first." This means that you must set priorities and meet deadlines.

For instance, if I am burning to work on a book but have a report due the next morning, I write the report first, get it done, and fax or e-mail it to the client. Then I reward myself with an afternoon spent on the book. If I indulged myself and worked on the book first, I'd risk not leaving myself enough time to get my report written by the deadline.

Another "Rule of the Office" worth quoting here is, Rule #2, "Make sure it's a working meeting." This rule reminds me to avoid meetings unless there is a set working agenda. A recent survey from NFO Research shows that the average business professional attends more than 60 meetings a month, and that U.S. employees now spend more than one-third of their time in meetings (*Continental* magazine, October, 1998).

But half of these meetings are unnecessary or inefficient. Before agreeing to attend a meeting, find out what topic(s) will be discussed and see if a solution can be reached without a formal meeting. Half of the problems usually can. Ben Stein, actor, novelist, and TV game show host, was once asked how he got so much accomplished. "It's simple," said Stein. "I don't go to meetings."

Meetings can be one of the biggest time-robbers. In his book *Team Up for Success* (AMI Publishing), Charles Caldwell gives the following tips for managing meeting time:

- Decide in advance when meetings will start and stop. Let participants know this information before the meeting begins.

- Start and stop on schedule. Start on time even if everyone isn't there.

- Schedule time blocks for each item to be discussed. Make sure meeting participants know how much time is allotted for each item.

- Keep track of time. Comments such as, "We have only 30 minutes left," help keep people on track.

> Want to make meetings shorter? Take the chairs out of the room! According to Allen Bluedorn, associate professor of management at the University of Missouri, meetings in which all participants stand are a third shorter than sit-down conferences—yet the decisions made in them are just as sound (*Psychology Today,* January/February, 1999).

Overcome procrastination

"Procrastination," says entrepreneur Victor Kiam, "is opportunity's assassin."

Procrastination is the single biggest factor causing people to fall behind in their work, miss deadlines, and turn in shoddy efforts. P.T. Barnum advised, "Never defer for a single hour that which can be done just as well now." Scientist Thomas Huxley noted, "No good is ever done by hesitation."

Having a daily to-do list—and then assigning yourself various tasks throughout the day in one-hour increments—helps you stay on track and avoid putting things off.

As long as you have your short-term deadlines and long-term goals in mind, you can be somewhat flexible in your daily schedule, adjusting tasks and time slots to match your enthusiasm for each project.

Breaking tasks into one-hour sessions, and then juggling the schedule to work on what interests you most right now, helps overcome procrastination: When you get tired or run out of ideas on one project, just switch to another.

Give yourself rewards for accomplishing tasks. If you work for a solid hour on a budget that's slow going, reward yourself with a break to read your mail or walk around the office building. If you stick with your schedule for the whole morning, treat yourself to your favorite food for lunch.

The best way to make every hour of every day productive is to have an hour-by-hour schedule. People who have such a schedule know what they should be doing every minute and, therefore, do it. People who don't set a schedule tend to drift through the day, stopping and then starting tasks, jumping from job to job, without getting much done.

As Henry Ford observed, "Nothing is particularly hard if you divide it into small jobs." Any project that seems overwhelming can be made less intimidating by breaking it into component parts, phases, or sections—and then working on these parts one at a time. In fact, the whole basis of project management is to break projects into tasks and tasks into activities. Then schedule each and do each small activity by the deadline on the schedule.

In the same way, virtually anyone can handle a series of one-hour jobs during the day with ease. Even four or five one-hour sessions in a day will get things done. Make the list of project steps, post it on your wall, and start step one. In his book *Scottish Proverbs* (Birlinn Limited), Colin S.K. Walker notes, "Half the battle with work is getting started."

Procrastinators frequently miss deadlines. They complete assignments at the last minute, allowing no time to review the work before handing it in. And they put themselves and their colleagues under undue stress.

Putting off unpleasant, routine, or difficult chores is human nature. But those who discipline themselves to tackle the things they dislike or fear gain self-confidence and make better use of their time.

The techniques below can help you overcome procrastination:

- Imagine how great you'll feel when the chore is completed. Think positively about its outcome.
- If the project is complex or overwhelming, break it down into a series of steps to be entered on your "Things To Do" list. Then set up a specific time and date to begin working on the first step, and follow through as if it were an appointment. Promise to spend 60 minutes a day on the task until it's done, and schedule these daily segments at the same time each day—preferably for a quiet period when there will be no interruptions.
- Create an incentive by promising yourself a special reward for getting the job done.

🕐 Realize the task doesn't have to be done perfectly. Some attempt is better than no attempt. Maybe you can get away with doing only part of the job and then passing it along to someone else for completion.

🕐 Delegate or outsource segments of the work you find boring or distasteful. You can gain precious hours, energy, and enthusiasm by passing along mundane, peripheral, or partly finished work to subordinates or co-workers. The more routine jobs you can delegate, the more time you'll have for other things.

So, don't procrastinate another second. Start attacking things now. "Putting off an easy thing makes it hard," observes George Claude Lorimer. "Putting off a hard thing makes it impossible."

Eliminate bad habits that waste time

First, identify any bad habits you have that waste your time. For me, it was sleeping an hour after I first woke up in the morning. Because the morning is the most productive work time for me, by forcing myself to get dressed and go to the office when I wake up, instead of falling back into bed, I increased my productivity tremendously.

For you, it may be watching a soap opera in the middle of the day, spending too much time surfing the Web, talking in chat rooms or on the phone, doing housework, or staying up too late at night to read or watch television.

After you have identified the bad habits, make a list of the ones you must avoid. Phrase each item on your list in the imperative voice. For example, if your worst time-wasting habit is procrastination, this should read as "Don't procrastinate" on your list. If you take on too many ancillary responsibilities because you hate saying no, this item should appear on your list as "Learn to say no."

Post this list in your office in a place where you will always see it, such as on the wall in front of you or on your bulletin board or door. Or place it in a desk drawer where you will see it every day. With this list of bad habits visible, you will be reminded constantly to avoid them and correct behaviors that waste time. Before long, you'll see a big improvement and will be getting more done in less time. Try it!

Avoid distractions

Outside distractions can be a major time-waster, if you let them. An outside distraction is any unscheduled activity that interrupts the task you are currently working on. For instance, if you're dedicated in the morning to working on a report, and a colleague asks you to call a customer to help resolve an immediate technical problem, that's an outside distraction.

The key is to physically block out disturbances as much as possible, whether by shutting your door, turning your desk away from passersby, letting your voice mail take your calls, posting a "do not disturb" sign, working at home for part of the day, or asking people to be quiet. Your mind can successfully tune out a great many signals if you tell it to.

If interruptions are a real problem, try setting aside a period every day during which you will meet with people and take phone calls. The rest of the time is "private time" in which you can work, uninterrupted. Most people say they accomplish more when they work on a task uninterrupted for as long as they want to.

The main idea is to do things on your schedule, rather than the schedules of others. It's not always possible. But the more you control your time, the more you'll be in control of your life.

Use the 80/20 rule

The 80/20 rule states that 80 percent of your accomplishments come from only 20 percent of your efforts. The trick is to figure out what makes that 20 percent so productive. Then, devote more of your time to these productive activities, and reduce time spent on unproductive work. To analyze how you spend your time, keep a log of your daily activities for about two weeks.

The next step is to find solutions to these time-wasters. Can you create form letters for replying to correspondence or have your secretary draft replies? Maybe you can create a convenient form that can be used to handle a particular type of communication, eliminating the need to draft a memo every time such an instance arises. Could you or an assistant clean up and organize the filing system? How about combining business trips, or scheduling travel time for off hours? For instance, scheduling an out-of-town trip for Monday morning permits you to fly out Sunday evening, so you don't lose part of a workday in travel.

Make and use standard operating procedures

Manufacturing mass-produced items is profitable and efficient because it's so cookie-cutter: Each widget is exactly like the one before it. That being the case, the steps in manufacturing all the widgets on the assembly line are the same. Therefore, these steps can be documented in writing, making them simple and easy to follow.

White-collar professionals can benefit from this essentially blue-collar productivity booster: Instead of reinventing the wheel each time, do what you did the last time you faced a similar situation. Or do something similar. Learn from repetition. Isolate the steps. Save components and parts (images, text, spreadsheets) you can reuse. Be as efficient as the factory line making widgets. Break each task into tiny steps. Write them down as a standard operating procedure. Refer to this document whenever you have to do the task.

Take customer service, for instance. Many customer service departments waste an enormous amount of time answering questions, especially from new customers, that they've answered over and over again. My friend David Yale has a neat solution.

First, survey your customer-service staff to find out the most common questions they get from new customers. Then answer these questions in a "welcome kit" that you send to all new customers. Your customer service burden should decrease, says Yale. The cost of the kit? Less than a dollar.

What else do you do that's routine and could be turned into a standard operating procedure? Get computer software and other tools to help you automate these processes. Don't engage in time-consuming problem solving when there's a recipe that could be followed more easily and more productively. If you had to make a pie, for instance, why would you perform chemical analysis of other pies to determine the compounds in the crust when you could just look it up in a cookbook? Yet people do the equivalent every day. What a waste!

You need not invent or document these procedures yourself, if you don't want to: There's a ton of them available from a variety of sources, yours for the asking. If you don't know how to do something—clean a fax machine, change your oil, fire an employee—go to the library, the bookstore, or the World Wide Web. Chances are the complete directions are already there, waiting for you to read and learn from them.

Adjust your schedule to your energy levels

Most of us have certain times during the day when we're most alert and perform better. Once you've determined your pattern of physical and mental energy levels, try to adjust your daily schedule to mesh with it. By handling mentally demanding jobs during your peak energy periods, you can get more done in less time. Fit your schedule to your moods and energy levels, and you'll find that you'll save time and be more effective in your job.

Most of us cannot control the hours we favor. Dr. Nathaniel Kleitman, a physiologist at the University of Chicago, says body temperature varies by up to three degrees during each day. When your body temperature drops, you have maximum energy. When it rises, your energy drops. (This may explain why, according to a recent survey, most people say they would rather be too cold than too hot.)

Dr. Emmanuel Mignot, co-author of a study published in the journal *Sleep*, says his research team may have found variations in a particular gene that determine whether you prefer to rise early or stay up late. Although further research is needed to confirm the finding, Mignot suggests that if it's true, work schedules in the future may be arranged so people handle the toughest tasks during periods when they are most likely to be productive (*The Record*, October 25, 1998).

So if you are a night owl, burning the midnight oil may result in maximum productivity for you. If you are an early bird, get up early and start working while everyone else in your house is still asleep.

Other people find that they can alter their circadian rhythm deliberately by changing when they go to bed and get up. If you have a choice of whether to be an early-morning person or a late-nighter, and your schedule allows you to do either, pick the one that works best for you.

If all else is equal, choose the morning. When you start early in the morning, as I do, you have the benefit of having completed a significant amount of your day's work quota by the time others are first stumbling into their offices. Early starters finish the day's work early and have the rest of the time to do more work or play. Late starters are behind from the moment they get up and feel increasing pressure to get their work done as the hour grows even later.

The easiest productivity tip in the world is to get up and start working an hour earlier than you normally do. Freelance writer Charles Flowers says whenever he has a deadline or a lot of work on a given day, he gets up as early as he must to meet that deadline, even if it means rising at 5 in the morning. I have, on some days, been at the office as early as 3 or 4 a.m., although this is rare.

Maintain peak energy during the day

Energy is a function of many factors, one of them being enthusiasm. When you are enthusiastic, your energy can remain high, even if you are physically tired. When you are bored, your energy drains, and you become lethargic and unproductive.

To maintain peak productivity and energy, maintain peak enthusiasm and avoid boredom. The main cause of boredom is not doing what you want, when you want to do it. Therefore, you should structure your work so you are spending most of your time doing what you want, when you feel like doing it.

Obviously, you should shy away from assignments that bore you. Forcing yourself to work on things you dislike will drain your energy. But even those assignments that interest you can get boring if you work on them for too long or if you don't feel like doing them at the time. The solution is to have many different projects and to work on the ones you want to work on at any given time. Because you largely set your own hourly schedule each day (meetings are an exception), you can do tasks in the order that pleases you, as long as you meet your deadlines.

Of course, when a deadline is looming, you may have no choice but to put aside work you want to do and focus on what has to be done to meet that deadline. But even this is avoidable if you negotiate sufficient deadlines and then plan your time so you get started early, rather than waiting until the last minute as so many people do.

Everyone finds something that can help revitalize them throughout the day. When you find what works for you, do it. My office has a private bathroom, and when I feel my concentration and energy waning, I wash my hair. I become immediately refreshed—perhaps the wet head of hair cools my overheated brain. You can take a break and re-energize by washing your face, taking a walk, running errands, meeting a friend for coffee, or chatting on the phone.

Design a productive workspace

A computer tech I recently hired to do some work for me commented, "I really like your computer system—everything is in easy reach." He then mentioned that in many personal computer systems, the owners put vital components, such as the CPU or disk drive or printer, on the floor, under a desk, or otherwise out of reach. I've seen that and I feel that it wastes effort and time. My philosophy is that everything you need—computer systems, office equipment, the telephone, supplies, reference materials, files—should be reachable just by swiveling your chair and reaching out to the appropriate cabinet, shelf, or drawer...without having to get out of your seat.

Plenty of desk space and file cabinet storage also boost productivity. All the materials I need—files, reference books, supplies, computer equipment, telephone, fax, copier—are right at hand. I can swivel in my chair or reach over to get what I need, without getting up and trekking across the room.

Make sure you have adequate space to organize and store work materials so they're close at hand and easy to find. Having to search for a book or folder wastes time and can cause you to lose your pace when you're in a productive groove. I have two desks and two large tables in my office, so there is plenty of surface space for various projects.

I recommend you design your workspace to minimize distractions and the need to get up. My office is on a quiet third floor of a small office building in northern New Jersey. At home, I am constantly interrupted by family members, neighbors, salespeople, and service personnel. Even on the busy first floor of this office building, there would be noise, delivery people knocking on the door and asking if I know where Mr. X's office is, and other interruptions. But almost no one comes to the third floor.

There is only one other office up here in addition to mine. It's quiet, and I can get a lot of work done. People who visit and see that I am almost alone and a walk up two flights of stairs think I must have gotten stuck with the worst office in the building. They don't realize I chose it deliberately.

> When you build your reference library, be generous, yet selective. This means don't acquire a book, CD ROM, or other reference material unless it relates to the subjects you work on. By the same token, if you see a book you know would be useful, buy it right then and there. Don't hesitate because of the price. It's a small investment to save valuable time later on getting information you need.

10 tips to help you work better and faster

1. Use a computer. Anyone in any business who wants to be productive (from the manager of an insurance company to a contractor scheduling appointments) should use a modern PC with the latest software. Doing so can double, triple, or even quadruple your output. Chapter 5 guides you on the technology you should acquire and how to use it.

2. Don't be a perfectionist. "I'm a non-perfectionist," said Isaac Asimov, author of 475 books. "I don't look back in regret or worry at what I have written." Be a careful worker, but don't agonize over your work beyond the point where the extra effort no longer produces a proportionately worthwhile improvement in your final product.

Be excellent but not perfect. Customers do not have the time or budget for perfection; for most projects, getting 95 to 98 percent of the way to perfection is good enough. That doesn't mean you deliberately make errors or give less than your best. It means you stop polishing and fiddling with the job when it looks good to you—and you don't agonize over the fact that you're not spending another hundred hours on it. Create it, check it, then let it go.

Understand the exponential curve of excellence. Quality improves with effort according to an exponential curve. That means that early effort yields the biggest results; subsequent efforts yield smaller and smaller improvements, until eventually the miniscule return is not worth the effort. Productive people stop at the point where the investment in further effort on a task is no longer justified by the tiny incremental improvement it would produce. Aim for 100-percent perfection and you are unlikely to be productive or profitable. Consistently hit within the 90 to 98 percent range and you will maximize both customer satisfaction as well as return on your time investment.

"Perfection does not exist," wrote Alfred de Musset. "To understand this is the triumph of human intelligence; to expect to possess it is the most dangerous kind of madness."

3. Free yourself from the pressure to be an innovator. As publisher Cameron Foote observes, "Clients are looking for good, not great." Do your best to meet the client's or your boss's requirements. They will be happy. Do not feel pressured to reinvent the wheel or create a masterpiece on every project you take on. Don't be held up by the false notion that you must uncover some great truth or present your boss with revolutionary ideas and concepts. Most successful business solutions are just common sense packaged to meet a specific need.

Eliminate performance pressure. Don't worry about whether what you are doing is different or better than what others have done before you. Just do the best you can. That will be enough.

4. Switch back and forth between different tasks. Even if you consider yourself a specialist, do projects outside your specialty. Inject variety into your schedule. Arrange your daily schedule so you switch off from one assignment to another at least once or twice each day. Variety, as the saying goes, is indeed the spice of life.

Approximately 70 to 90 percent of what I am doing at any time is in tasks within my area of expertise. This keeps me highly productive. The other 10 to 30 percent is in new areas, markets, industries, or disciplines outside my area of expertise. This keeps me fresh and allows me to explore things that captivate my imagination but are not in my usual schedule of assignments.

5. Don't waste time working on projects you don't have yet. Get letters of agreement, contracts, purchase orders, and budget sign-offs before proceeding. Don't waste time starting the work for projects that may not come to fruition. An official approval or go-ahead from your boss or from a customer makes the project real and firm, so you can proceed at full speed with the confidence and enthusiasm that come from knowing you have been given the green light.

6. Make deadlines firm but adequate. Of 150 executives surveyed by AccounTemps, 37 percent rated the dependable meeting of deadlines as the most important quality of a team player (*Continental* magazine, October, 1997).

Productive people set and meet deadlines. Without a deadline, the motivation to do a task is small to nonexistent. Tasks without assigned deadlines automatically go to the bottom of your priority list. After all, if you have two reports to file—and one is due a week from Thursday, and the other due "whenever you can get around to it"—which do you suppose will get written first?

Often you will collaborate with your supervisor or customer in determining deadlines. Set deadlines for a specific date and time, not a time period. For example, "due November 23 by 3 p.m. or sooner," not "in about two weeks." Having a specific date and time for completion eliminates confusion and gives you motivation to get the work done on time.

At the same time, don't make deadlines too tight. Try to build in a few extra days for the unexpected, such as a missing piece of information, a delay from a subcontractor, a last-minute change, or a crisis on another project.

7. Protect and value your time. Productive people guard their time more heavily than the gold in Fort Knox. They don't waste time. They get right to the point. They may come off as abrupt or dismissive to some people. But they realize they cannot give everyone who contacts them all the time each person wants. They determine how much time to spend with each person. They make decisions. They say what needs to be said, do what needs to be done, and then move on.

Respect hour power. One successful entrepreneur told me he doesn't wear a watch and never knows what time it is. But he's the exception, not the rule. Most busy and successful people I've met are aware of the relentless pressure of time. And they keep track of it like they would watch a limited inventory of a precious raw material in a manufacturing plant. If you watch successful, experienced poker players, they will carefully divide money into piles of coins and bills, sorted by denomination. Successful time managers divide their days into hourly increments in much the same way. And spend them even more carefully.

Think of your time this way: Assign a dollar value to each hour. Whether staff or independent, salaried or hourly, every productive person can tell you the worth of his or her time. Let's say you mow lawns for a living and can do two lawns per hour. If your fee is $15 per lawn, the hour value of your time is $30. Productive people weigh the effort required for specific activities—and the return it will produce—against the cost of the time based on the dollar value of their hour. Maybe the lawn professional wants to add hedge-clipping as a service. If he can charge $20 per hedge and do four in an hour, that's an $80-an-hour return. Based on his current hourly worth of $30, it's an extremely profitable move.

8. Stay focused. As Robert Ringer (the bestselling author of *Looking Out For #1*) observes, successful people apply themselves to the task at hand. They work until the work gets done.

They concentrate on one or two things at a time. They don't go in a hundred different directions. My experience is that people who are big talkers—constantly spouting ideas or proposing deals and ventures—are spread out in too many different directions to be effective. Efficient people have a vision and focus their activities to achieve that vision.

To focus on what you do best, make only what you add value to—and buy the rest around the corner. A member of the X-Men, my son's favorite team of super heroes, frequently comments, "I'm the best there is at what I do" (in his case, it's beating bad guys). Productive workers spend their time doing what they do better and faster than anyone else. To gain more of these profitable hours, they outsource and delegate other tasks to vendors and subordinates. There are endless ways to spend your time, if you want to pursue them all. Unfortunately, your time is anything but endless. Productivity means selectivity. Don't attempt to do everything. You can't even come close, so why bother?

9. Set a production goal. Stephen King writes 1,500 words every day except on his birthday, Christmas, and the Fourth of July. Steinway makes 800 pianos in its German plant every year.

Workers and organizations who want to meet deadlines and be successful set a production goal and achieve it. An individual who truly wants to be productive sets a production goal, meets it, and then *keeps going* until he or she can do no more—or runs out of time—for the day.

Joe Lansdale, author of *Bad Chili* (Mysterious Press) and many other novels, says he never misses his productivity goal of writing three pages a day, five days a week. "I'm not in the mood; I don't feel like it; what kind of an excuse is that?" Lansdale said in an interview with *Publishers Weekly* (September 29, 1997). "If I'm not in the mood, do I not go to the chicken plant if I've got a job in the chicken plant?"

10. Do work you enjoy. In advising people on choosing their life's work, David Ogilvy, founder of the advertising agency Ogilvy & Mather, quotes a Scottish proverb that says, "Be happy while you're living; for you're a long time dead." The *Tao Te Ching* says, "In work, do what you enjoy."

When you enjoy your work, it really isn't work. To me, success is being able to make a good living while spending the workday in pleasurable tasks. You won't love every project equally, of course. But try to balance "must-do" mandatory tasks with things that are more fun for you. Seek assignments that are exciting, interesting, and fulfilling.

In addition to enjoying their work, many super-productive people gain enjoyment from the act of being super-productive itself. These people aren't necessarily workaholics. But they are proud of their accomplishments—and their efficiency. My definition of a productive, efficient person is someone who can do in a day what others take a week to accomplish.

Talk to super-productive people. Many get a rush out of being super-efficient time managers, in addition to the pleasure they derive from simply being competent in their job, profession, or skill set. I love doing good work. But I also get a thrill out of doing two projects in a week when my colleagues are only doing one.

Can you train yourself to like work better and enjoy it more? Motivational experts say we have the ability to change our attitudes and behavior. "Attitude is a trap or it is freedom. Create your own," writes Judy Crookes in *Inner Realm* magazine (August 1998).

Whatever your motivation, use it to enjoy not only having a good job, but doing the work itself. My motivation is avoiding boredom. Every day that I come into my office and turn on the computer I'm thankful that I can make a good living writing, and therefore don't have to do some other job that would bore me.

Many professionals in all fields love their work so much, they never stop. English major Lee Falk, for example, created The Phantom, which was recently made into a feature film, in 1936. Six decades later, Falk, in his 80s, was still writing the comic strip, which appears daily.

"Enjoy your achievements as well as your plans," advised Max Ehrmann in his 1927 essay "Desiderata." "Keep interested in your own career, however humble; it is a real possession in the changing fortunes of time."

Mark Gruenwald, a senior editor at Marvel Comics, loved his work so much that when he died in 1996, he left a request that his ashes be mixed into the ink used to reprint a superhero series he had written. According to an article in the *Daily News* (August 29, 1997), his wish was granted. "He has truly become one with the story," said his widow, Catherine Gruenwald.

One other point: Achieving a noticeable increase in personal productivity needn't be a quantum leap or radical change. Just adapt two or three of the suggestions in this chapter. Practice them on a daily basis. In no time, you will begin to see light at the end of the tunnel of busyness—and the picture will only get brighter from there.

Chapter 2

Do You Really Want to Be Productive?

"Time is a precious possession and I attempt to make the most of it by not wasting it, for it is irreplaceable."
—Stanley Marcus, *Minding the Store*
(University of N. Texas Press, 1998)

If you want to be superproductive, there are certain things you will have to give up. These things include the extravagant luxuries of sloth, inertia, laziness, and wasted idle time. If you are not willing to give these up, you must seriously question whether being more productive is truly a priority in your life. If it isn't, that's okay. However, don't complain that there's "never enough time," and then watch 25 hours of sports on TV each weekend.

The primary reason most workers are not productive is that they do not really desire it. Isaac Asimov wanted to write a lot of books, and so he designed his life to increase his output (this included focusing on topics on which he could produce books quickly and avoiding travel, so he could spend most of his time in his study). This chapter presents guidelines to help you assess whether being productive is important to you, and whether you are willing to do what is necessary to achieve superior productivity.

Set your goals high

Many workers who are ambitious look at other workers, see what they produce, and set their own goals slightly higher.

Unfortunately, this won't make you productive. The majority of workers have limited outputs. So even if you do 10 percent more, your output will still be small.

Do not use the average worker as a role model for productivity. Most people do not set their sights high enough. For instance, upon hearing that a famous novelist was coming out with his first new novel in half a decade, Stephen King once commented, "Come on...it doesn't take five years to write a novel."

We productive workers want to get the job done, polish it, and move on to the next task. We care about quality, but we strive for excellence rather than perfection.

I've found that productive professionals admire other productive people precisely because these workers are productive. In his autobiography *It Came From Ohio!* (Scholastic Books), R.L. Stine, author of 250 books, comments, "I read an article about a writer in South America who has written over a thousand books! Sometimes he writes three books a day! My hero!"

Stine, incidentally, says he works six or seven days a week to write two books every month. Isaac Asimov worked seven days a week from 7:30 a.m. to 10:30 p.m., stopping only for business lunches, social engagements, telephone conversations, and other activities he referred to as "interruptions."

Although you don't have to be a workaholic to be a productive worker, it does help. Most workers who are more productive than their peers work more than just from 9 to 5. Claude Hopkins, one of the most successful advertising executives of all time, said he got twice as much accomplished as everyone else in his agency because he worked twice as hard and twice as long.

Thomas Edison, the productive inventor, bragged about being a workaholic who only slept four or five hours a night. Frank Reich, the inventor of Tufoil motor oil additive, told me that while he was in the throes of pursuing his invention, he moved a cot into his lab so he could sleep there and not waste time going back and forth.

I am not telling you to be a workaholic or sacrifice the rest of your life. But in a sense, to be productive at anything, some sacrifices must be made. Entrepreneur Andrew Linick points out that everything we want—everything we want to do, learn, achieve, or create—has a price. And that price is *time*. Productive workers pay this price to be productive. If you're not willing to pay it, there's a limit to what you can do.

Set realistic, but ambitious, goals. Do not be afraid to take on challenges and try new things. "In order to succeed at almost anything, it's necessary to risk failure at various times along the way," advises Dr. Joyce Brothers in her newspaper column (New York's *Daily News*, April 10, 1996).

"If you stay committed, your dreams can come true," says Michael Blake, who wrote the movie *Dances With Wolves*. "I left home at 17 and had nothing but rejections for 25 years. I wrote more than 20 screenplays, but I never gave up."

Enjoy your work

The majority of Americans really dislike their work. "Everybody but a complete idiot or a college professor who has never had a lick of work in their lives looks forward to quitting time, and the sooner it comes the better," a factory worker told Benjamin Hunnicutt, author of *Kellogg's Six-Hour Day* (Temple University Press, 1996). But as Marilyn Machlowitz observes in her book *Workaholics* (New American Library, 1980), "When work is a joy and not just a job, it is never odious or arduous."

🕐 Learn to like the work you do. If you find something you enjoy and are good at, you will not be able to stop long enough to get a good night's sleep.

37

⊕ Psychologist Mihaly Csikszentmihalyi has coined the term "flow" to describe the state of mind people are in when they love their work. According to this theory, flow is a state in which people are so involved in an activity that nothing else seems to matter; the experience is so enjoyable that people will do it even at great cost (*Flow*, HarperCollins, 1991). If you've ever been so wrapped up in what you were doing that you didn't want to stop, you were probably in flow. The more you are in flow, the more you will enjoy work, and the more productive you will be.

⊕ Naturalist Sigurd Olson comments, "Give me work which I like to do." The question he asks himself to determine whether he can be productive in a job: "Can I lose myself in this work, wrap my entire being up in it...or will it be just another job again?" (Quoted in *A Wilderness Within: The Life of Sigurd F. Olson* by David Backes, University of Minnesota Press, 1997)

⊕ Herb Kelleher, CEO of Southwest Airlines, says, "I work most of the time. I enjoy what I do. My vocation is my avocation. If you enjoy what you do there's no stress connected to it. Every day is a pleasure." (Cited in *Computerworld*, September 28, 1998). Winston Churchill once said, "Those whose work and pleasures are one are fortune's favorite children."

Value your time

Almost everyone complains about not having enough time. Yet the way many people act shows they place almost no value on their time. That's contradictory and a shame.

Everyone's time has value. To understand this value and make it meaningful, you need to assign an actual dollar-per-hour value to your time. Then, when you make decisions about how to spend your time, you weigh the hourly cost against the potential reward from the activity you're considering. If it doesn't pay off, don't do it.

For instance, my wife has a friend, Mary, who spends a lot of her time driving to different stores to hunt down the best sales.

She proudly boasts about saving $1 on paper towels or getting a product that costs $25 at the nearby mall for only $16 at a discount outlet 15 miles away.

To Mary, this represents real savings and a source of pride. To me, it's a waste of time. When you factor in time spent, gas, tolls, and the wear-and-tear on Mary's car, the so-called bargain is no bargain at all. To me, that's too high a price to pay to "save" a few dollars. But Mary sees money in absolute terms. She doesn't factor in the value of her time.

How do you assign a dollar value to your time? If you are self-employed and charge by the hour for your services, the worth of your time readily apparent. Likewise, hourly employees have a clear picture of the worth of their time: If they earn $14.88 an hour, wasting an hour costs $14.88.

My lawyer, for example, charges $200 an hour. Instead of taking an hour to go to a discount mall and save $9, he could spend the hour doing billable work and make $200. Even if he misses out on the discount savings, he comes out $191 ahead for the hour.

Even if you don't charge or get paid by the hour, your time still has a dollar value. Calculating it is easy. If you are paid $50,000 a year, your time is worth about $1,000 a week. If you put in a 40-hour week, that comes to $25 an hour. When you are tempted into a nonessential activity, keep that $25-an-hour figure in mind. That's what it costs to waste an hour.

Take coupons, for example. People I know can't understand why I don't use coupons when buying groceries at the supermarket. "You're paying too much!" they exclaim. "You could get it cheaper!" They don't understand that it's not just money that has a value; time does too. When I calculate the time and energy required to look for, clip, save, file, retrieve, search for products, and remember to use coupons, it's not worth it to me.

Last week in the supermarket, I was picking up a package of butter when a man tapped me on the shoulder. "Don't buy that now," he advised me in a friendly tone. "Come back tomorrow. It will be on sale—one dollar off."

I smiled, thanked him for the information—and bought the butter. To go back to the store tomorrow, rather than buy the butter on the spot, would take at least 20 minutes. Is my time or yours truly worth only $3 an hour? That's apparently what my butter-bargain-hunting friend believes. I don't.

My wife, Amy, doesn't always agree with this idea of weighing the dollar value of time against the dollar savings or costs of the alternatives. One morning, when my car was at the repair station for service, she objected to my plan to call a taxi to take me to work. "Relax," I said. "My office is only two miles away and the ride costs about $6."

"Why waste $6?" she replied. "I have the mini-van. I'll drop you off when I take the kids to school."

"That won't get me to the office until 8:45," I objected. "The taxi will get me there by 7:30. If I wait for you, I'll lose over an hour of productive work time."

She fumed and protested, but I took a cab anyway. At the time, my billing rate for my consulting service was a couple of hundred dollars an hour. Yet Amy saw the $6 cab ride as a waste of money. Two different mind-sets. If you want to be superproductive, follow mine.

Here are some suggestions for making the most profitable use of your time:

1. Work on critical tasks when you are freshest and most energetic. For me, this is the earlier part of the day—from 7 a.m. until about 1 p.m.

2. If you are very busy this week, don't even leaf through the journals and magazines that come across your desk. Instead, throw them out.

3. Tell people who make social calls that you are too busy to talk and that you will call them back when you're free.

4. When you get tired of working on a project, don't force yourself to continue (unless under deadline). Instead, put it aside and work on something else.

5. Try to conduct your activities from your office rather than making trips. Travel can be an enormous time waster. Travel as much as you have to, but no more. If a transaction can be handled just as effectively via phone, fax, or e-mail, do it.

6. Try to eliminate unproductive activities that may be fun but don't lighten your workload. Years ago I gave up college teaching because it was taking away too much time. Be wary of taking on volunteer work just because someone asks you to.

7. Try getting up earlier and putting in an extra hour every morning from Monday through Friday. That's five extra hours of productive time a week.

8. If you are going to work on the weekend, early Saturday morning is a good time. You can get in an extra three to five hours and still have the rest of the weekend free.

Know the value of time and money

Do you need money? Most of us do. Unless you are independently wealthy or have a second source of income, most workers need to earn a paycheck to pay rent or mortgage, health insurance premiums, utility bills, grocery and doctor bills, and for video rentals.

My father once told me, "Money is not important, as long as you're happy." But I disagree. I share the view of consultant Ted Nicholas. Writing in his *Direct Marketing Success Letter* (April 23, 1997), Ted says, "The happiest possible life ideally rests on a balance between four elements: health, career, personal relationships, and money."

Unfortunately, most workers don't have as much personal wealth as they desire. Why is it that so many Americans, even those with executive positions, have such a relatively low net worth? Because they spend too much. Americans are notoriously behind the rest of the world when it comes to accruing wealth. The average American family saves less than 5 percent of its earnings each year, compared with nearly 10 percent in the U.K. and almost 13 percent in Sweden.

Productive workers that I have met tend to be partially money-driven or at least money-conscious. They are not content with the meager income of the average worker. They may not all aspire to great wealth, but they all want to be comfortable. My definition of success is: Doing what you want, when and where you want to do it, *and getting paid well for it—sometimes very, very well.* This is what you can achieve when you are productive and put your nose to the grindstone, your back into your hammer swings, or your fingertips to the computer keys.

A wise person once remarked, "If you don't know where you are going, you are certainly never going to get there." Think about where you're going. How much money do you want? If you answer "enough" or "a lot," you haven't clearly defined your income goals. Without knowing where you are going, how will you get there? An important first step toward increasing your income is to set a specific dollar goal.

The purpose of setting this goal is not necessarily to meet it but to provide a target upon which all your efforts can be focused. Even if you do not earn the specific dollar figure, just having a goal and working toward it can increase your earnings far beyond what you would make just aimlessly plodding along. A goal gives you something to set your sights on, inspires hard work, and is a catalyst for success.

Leo Burnett, founder of the advertising agency that created the "Marlboro Man," is credited with the following observation: "If you reach for the stars and fall, you will get the moon. But if you reach just for a tree branch and fall, you will end up in the mud." In other words, it's always better to set your goals a little higher, a little beyond your reach, rather than make them too easy. The goal should be difficult, because success requires hard work and a bit of ambition. If you set easy goals, you will always achieve them, but you'll always achieve below your potential as well.

Another story illustrates this point: Two salespeople decide at the beginning of the year that they will set sales goals. Each writes his goal on a sheet of paper. At the end of the year, they meet.

The first salesman opens his paper and says to the second, "See, here is my goal: $50,000 in sales commissions. And I have done it. I achieved my goal!" He turns to his friend. "And how did you do?"

"Not as well," confesses the second salesman. "I set my goal at $1 million in sales commissions—and I, unlike you, have achieved only half of my goal."

You get the point?

Self-assessment test: Are you a productive worker?

Respond to these statements honestly. Then score yourself and check your rating.

1. I am a perfectionist. I redo work many times, because everything I do must be perfect.
   ❏ True ❏ False

2. I consider my finished work as a product unto itself, not an ends to satisfy a customer or supervisor.
   ❏ True ❏ False

3. It's very important to me to be well paid and successful at work.
   ❏ True ❏ False

4. I would sometimes rather be at the office working than at home doing household chores or leisure activities.
   ❏ True ❏ False

5. I would be bored at work if I had too little to do.
   ❏ True ❏ False

6. Being busy and productive is important to my ego and self-esteem.
   ❏ True ❏ False

7. I find myself constantly keeping track of my productivity, output, and accomplishments.
   ❏ True ❏ False

8. The fact that I am so productive is the thing people tend to notice most about me, and I like that very much.
   ❏ True ❏ False

9. My ego is tied to my work. When I have too few projects to do or am waiting to find out whether a big project is going to get the go-ahead from management, I get antsy.
   ❏ True ❏ False

Scoring: On questions 1 and 2, give yourself one point for every false answer, zero points for every true answer. On questions 3 through 9, give yourself one point for every true answer, zero points for every false answer. The more points you have, the closer your personality, attitude, and beliefs are to those of most workers who are productive.

If after answering these questions, you feel you have the personality of a high-productivity worker, don't fight it. The only way you are going to be really happy is if you are busy and productive. This book shows how to increase your output as well as your income.

On the other hand, if after taking the test you feel you don't fit the profile of the productive worker, stop and ask yourself "Is being productive really important to me? Is making a lot of money really important to me?" If the answer is no, maybe you'd be happier slowing down, being less frantic, and doing your work at a more leisurely pace. But if the answer is yes, how are you going to reconcile your desire to be productive with the fact that you don't share the same attitudes toward work as productive workers? You will either have to change some of your attitudes or habits or strike a balance between the desire to be productive and successful at work and the desire to spend more of your time at home relaxing.

Avoid job burnout

If you decide to pursue greater productivity, be aware of the possibility of burnout. While being a productive worker can be fulfilling, as human beings we have limits to our energy. If you work too hard, for too long without a break, you can become tired, fall out of "flow," and feel bored, de-energized, even depressed.

You can't always tell when job burnout strikes. In many instances people who feel unhappy or depressed are not able to pinpoint the reason. But job burnout victims often share many of the following feelings and circumstances:

   🕐 *Boredom.* Every now and then we all have a day when we'd rather be strolling in the park than be stuck in the office. That's only natural. But people experiencing job burnout are bored almost all the time. They are turned off by their assignments and have little enthusiasm for the job.

Job burnout is a stressful situation. It's no fun having to wake up each morning knowing you have to go to a job you despise. The symptoms of stress are different for different people, but be alert to symptoms like nervousness, fatigue, sleeplessness, heartburn, headaches, stomach aches, and constipation. They may be a sign that you are suffering stress caused by job burnout.

🕐 *Overworked.* Do you work too hard? Do you feel pressured by time, by deadlines? Do you say things like, "I wish there were 26 hours in the day"? If so, watch out! Overworked people are likely to suffer fatigue and stress that can eventually lead to job burnout.

🕐 *Underworked.* Surprisingly, being underworked is even more likely to lead to burnout than being overworked. The fact is, most people want to work and feel as if they're contributing something to the company. If you're not working at your full potential, you'll feel unproductive and unsatisfied.

One woman recently hired by a government agency complained to me, "I beg for more projects at work, but the supervisors just won't give them to me. I feel like I'm wasting my time. What's the point of being at work eight hours a day if I can complete my assignments by 10:30 in the morning?"

After only six months on the job, this woman is already sending out resumes and looking for a new position. She hopes to land a job with private industry where, she feels, her talents will be put to better use—and she'll avoid job burnout.

🕐 *Time consciousness.* Do you find yourself glancing at your watch more than four times an hour? Have you ever thought that an hour had gone by, but when you looked at your watch, it had been only five minutes? Does the second hand on the clock seem to move too slowly these days?

Job burnout victims are often extremely time conscious, but in a negative sense. They use the progression of time to help get them through the day, rather than to make the day more productive. And, they find that time on the job passes much more slowly than time at home. People who enjoy their work, on the other hand, find that the business day passes quickly.

🕐 *Difficulty concentrating.* When you enjoy what you're doing, it's easy to tackle the work with enthusiasm and vigor. But job burnout victims have a hard time applying themselves to their work because they find it boring and unfulfilling. If you find yourself staring at the same piece of paper for hours...or reading the same paragraph over and over...or you constantly feel drained and drowsy during the day...you may be a prime candidate for burnout.

🕐 *Low self-esteem.* According to the American work ethic, you are what you do. So if you don't think much of what you do, you won't think much of yourself.

Job burnout victims can get caught in a vicious cycle of self-degradation. Because they're dissatisfied with their job, they think work is a waste of time. And then they feel worthless because they think they're failures in their careers. Making this situation even worse is the fact that some people have an uncanny knack for sensing when others are feeling low and take advantage. This makes those at their lowest point resent themselves and their jobs even more.

🕐 *Withdrawn.* As self-esteem sinks lower and lower, burnout victims become overly introverted and withdrawn. They don't socialize or communicate with co-workers because of their work-inflicted inferiority complex. They look at co-workers who are seemingly satisfied with their jobs and say to themselves, "These people are doing okay. So it must be me, not the company or the job."

🕐 *Can't face the day.* A close friend of mine found he was spending every business morning hanging over the toilet throwing up. The thought of going to work was that distasteful to him. If getting out of bed to face the workday is an agonizing struggle, you probably have an advanced case of job burnout.

Okay. Let's say you think you're suffering from job burnout—either a mild or a severe case. What do you do about it? Here are 10 ways to avoid and overcome job burnout.

1. Ask for more work. Not getting a chance to work to your full potential is one of the biggest reasons for job burnout.

Why don't managers delegate more to their staffs? One reason is that they never learned how: most managers are doers, not delegators. Another reason is that a poor manager makes him- or herself feel more important by hogging all the work and leaving staffers in the dark.

Working under a manager who refuses to delegate makes people feel frustrated and useless. If you're not being used to your fullest potential, *ask for more work.* Tell your supervisor that you can tackle more...and that you want more to tackle.

"But I'm not sure you can handle more," your manager may reply. Fine, you say. I'll prove I can. Tell your manager to increase your workload just a little bit at first. Once he or she sees how efficiently and quickly you complete the assignment, you'll be given as much as you can handle.

Unfortunately, some managers are never going to delegate. If you're stuck working for one of them, changing jobs may be your only way out. (We'll take a look at that option a little later on.)

2. Take on different work. People joke about being stuck in a rut. But it's no joke. One business executive I know defines a rut as "a grave without a cover." Life shouldn't be a grind. It should be enjoyable, fun...even thrilling.

So if you feel stuck in a rut, get out. Break your daily routine by doing something new. For example, if you've always wanted to write but never tried it, volunteer to write an article for your company newsletter or a trade journal. If you've always thought sales would be fun but never tried it, volunteer to staff the booth at your company's next trade show exhibit. If you're interested in computers but haven't had much chance to work with them, sign up for your company's in-plant course in Unix or Excel.

3. Learn something new. Some people spend their professional lives rehashing and reworking the same limited bits of knowledge they picked up in school and their early training. For instance, an advertising writer I know complained to me that because he had become a specialist in automobiles, he had essentially written and rewritten the same set of ads for a dozen different clients over the course of his 25-year career.

Of course, he could have broken out of this at any time. He could have studied a new area to write about, such as consumer electronics, or soap, or medical products. But he didn't. And the longer he stayed within the narrow confines of automotive copywriting, the harder it became for him to try anything new.

Life and work become dull when you stop learning. So don't. Make it a point to broaden your knowledge, master new skills, and learn new things. For example, instead of throwing away college catalogs and course solicitations you receive in the mail, sign up for a course in a new topic that interests you. Or, if you don't have time for night school, you can always read a book or attend a lecture.

Rehashing the same database of knowledge you've always carried around in your brain is safe and easy. But it's also boring and can lead to job burnout. When you're continually learning new things about your work, you keep the interest and excitement level high.

4. Do something new. Go on a cruise. Learn to play the clarinet. Build a cedar closet.

This new thing that you try doesn't have to be work-related. The simple act of doing something you've never done before will boost your spirits and give you a new outlook on life—a positive attitude that will spill over onto your job.

By continually trying new things, you become well-rounded. And well-rounded people are the most content personally and professionally.

5. Become more active in your own field. Somewhere along the way, you may have lost the zest for engineering, science, sales, retail, or business that you had when you first started. The daily grind of nine-to-five has worn you down. And you've forgotten why you became an engineer, a photographer, or whatever it is you do, in the first place.

You can escape job burnout by rekindling your interest in your profession. Join your professional society, if you haven't already. Become active: attend meetings, read journals, present papers. You can even run for office in your local chapter. Take a course or teach one. Take responsibility for training one of the new employees in your department. The people who are active in their field are usually the most successful and the most satisfied with their careers.

6. Restructure your job. A secretary at an advertising agency explained to me the source of her career blues.

"I took a secretary-level job to get my 'foot in the door' in the advertising business. Although this is my first job in advertising, I have a pretty extensive writing background, mainly in employee communications for several large firms.

"I thought that in an ad agency I'd get an opportunity to put my writing skills to use. But it has not worked out that way. I know I could write very good copy, if I was given a chance. But my boss thinks of me strictly as a secretary and he has never given me the opportunity to use my talent to write an ad or a commercial."

Perhaps you too have been forced into a role against your will. Maybe you had hopes of doing "creative" projects but found yourself handling dry, routine procedures day after day. If you're unhappy with your job as it is, you can solve the problem by redefining your role in the organization.

First, look for things that need doing but that aren't being done. Then volunteer to take this work on. For example, let's say you're a technical manager who would rather be doing something else like computer programming. If your department needs to develop engineering software and you're fluent in Visual BASIC, you could take responsibility for writing the programs. As your department's need for customized technical programs grows, more and more of your time could be devoted to writing the software. By satisfying a need, you've also restructured your job to suit your tastes.

Of course, you can't always write your own job description. Some bosses won't allow it. And neither will some corporate structures. If that's the case, more drastic action (like finding a new job) may be needed to get your career back on track.

7. Attack problem co-workers head-on. "All this sounds nice, but not realistic," you complain. "My problem isn't just me; it's the people I work with." Fine. Then you need to assess that source of your job burnout and attack it head-on.

For example, maybe your life is being made miserable by a co-worker who simply refuses to cooperate with you. The two of you are supposed to be working on some of the same projects, sharing information and ideas. But your "partner" is a loner who always gives you the cold shoulder whenever you try to get together.

Confrontation is unpleasant, so you could remain silent and try to make the best of it. But you won't be solving the problem; you'll just be running away. And you'll only grow more miserable as a bad situation stays bad.

The better tactic is to confront the uncooperative co-worker head on. Tell your co-worker you have a problem you want to discuss in private. Then, tell him or her your feelings. Explain that you want to do a good job but you can't unless the two of you can find a way to work together productively and without friction. Be direct. Say, "It seems that whenever I approach you, you're not available. Have I done something to make you hesitant to work with me? Is there a way we can get together on this?"

In many cases, the source of our unhappiness at work is another person—a person who is making life difficult for us. By confronting difficult people with the fact that they are being difficult, you force them to admit their poor behavior and take steps to correct it. Which makes life easier for everyone.

8. Change departments. Sometimes, you can't change the person who is creating a problem for you. Or there may not be another job or task in your department that can provide you with career satisfaction. In that case, changing departments may be the answer.

This is a fairly common occurrence in industry. For example, engineers who would rather deal with people than equations can move into technical sales. Or a telecommunications specialist who is bored with phones but fascinated by computers might switch to the IS (information systems) department.

9. Change employers. If there's no place in your company where you would be happy, then maybe you should change your employer entirely. The unfortunate fact of professional life is that many places are simply horrible to work in; many bosses are despotic tyrants; and many companies are very poorly managed. If you're in one of these places, the best thing that you can do is to get out as soon as possible. But be sure to keep your job-hunting a secret. And don't quit your present job until you get a new one.

On the other hand, don't rush your resume to the printer at the first sign of trouble. Changing jobs is a major step. Are you sure your that the problem cannot be solved by less drastic measures, such as a change of assignment, a heart-to-heart talk with the boss, or a week's vacation? Before quitting, try and make things work out. Only when you're convinced that you can't improve your present situation should you put yourself back on the job market.

10. Change fields. Changing careers is an effective cure for severe job burnout. If you've had it with what you do for a living, maybe you should do something else.

There are a number of reasons why people hesitate to choose this option. One is the feeling that they studied for a specific career and they'd be wasting their education if they moved into a field for which they were not formally trained. But that's faulty reasoning. The real and tragic waste is working at a job that no longer fulfills you.

The second reason for hesitation is financial. People worry that they'll have to take a severe pay cut when they switch fields because they'll be starting at entry level. But that's not always the case. True, you may not make as much as you're making now. But you'll probably earn enough to maintain your present lifestyle. If not, perhaps your savings can see you through for the year or two it takes to reach a respectable salary in your new profession.

The third factor that keeps people stuck is that they fear radical change. But the change doesn't have to be radical; it can, in fact, be small. For example, a technical writer who is sick and tired of turning out operating manuals doesn't have to join the circus to find happiness. Maybe a different type of writing—say, newspaper reporting—will be enough of a change to break the career doldrums.

The decision to change jobs or professions should be made only after a lot of careful thought and soul searching. But change of some kind is definitely called for when you're stuck with a bad case of job burnout. After all, you spend more than a third of your waking hours at your job. Doesn't it make sense to have a job you like?

> To avoid job burnout, publisher Dan Poynter recommends taking a week's vacation or getting involved in a totally new activity. Rest and relaxation can help recharge you when you feel burnout coming on. If you have young kids, take a week's vacation with them. If you have a significant other, travel to an exotic, romantic, or exciting place. Or, do a sport or an activity that always interested you but that you never had time for.

The bottom line: If you want to be more efficient and are willing to work at it, you will succeed. If you're not enthusiastic about getting more done and having more time for yourself, you probably won't change the current practices that are keeping you from being fully productive.

Chapter 3

The 10% Solution for Increased Personal Efficiency

"We're moving to a culture where everything moves faster, where no one has any time, where we measure out our days not in coffee spoons but in e-mails, beeper buzzes, timed phone calls, children's scheduled play dates, and vacations with cell phones and laptops at hand."

—Esther Dyson, author of *Release 2.0* (Broadway Books, 1997)

Master musicians may have to practice many hours a day, day after day, for a year or more to slightly enhance their skills. In fact, their skill level is so high, they might have to practice this much just to maintain it, let alone improve it. One classical musician commented, "If I don't practice for a day, I know it. If I don't practice for two days, my wife knows it. If I don't practice for three days, the audience knows it."

But when it comes to increasing our own personal efficiency, few of us are masters or even close. Therefore, we can achieve significant improvements in our personal productivity—10 to 25 percent or more—without enormous effort. This chapter out-lines incremental improvements so you can make tiny "baby steps" that will take little effort, but yield big results.

Feel the power of 10% more

Stand up. Reach as high as you can. Notice where your hand is? Okay. Now put your hand 6 inches higher.

If you're like most people at my personal productivity semi-nars, you achieved the increase by standing on your chair or desk. Standing on tiptoes is another favorite method.

The point is simple: The first time we try anything, we usu-ally don't put forth our total effort. So we fall short. To increase your results, then, you can put forth a little more effort than you normally do, just by reminding yourself that's what you need to do to achieve the increased productivity you want.

Let's say you make widgets. You make 50 widgets each hour. Could you do 10 percent more...55 an hour? Probably. Almost certainly. So turn up your motor and do it! You won't need to revolutionize your production methods or gain super-human speed. Just work at it a bit harder.

You'll find it's pretty easy to do 10 percent more of almost anything. Yet this simple effort pays big dividends. In our exam-ple, if you work an 8-hour day in your widget shop, a 10-percent improvement will increase yield by 10,000 widgets a year. If your profit is $10 a unit, that's an extra $100,000 in annual profit.

The 10 percent solution can improve your productivity in several different areas. The rest of this chapter will apply the formula to these areas and then offer practical suggestions for implementing the plan.

Increase efficiency 10%

Do you feel pressured? Do you feel like you don't have enough time even to breathe during the day? "Yes," you may be thinking. But it probably isn't really so. If you don't believe me, try this experiment.

Set up a video camera. Point it at your desk. Turn it on. Tape yourself working. Then watch the tape.

To your amazement, you'll see yourself daydreaming, sitting at your desk staring into space, chatting idly with colleagues, making prolonged personal calls, drinking coffee, fussing with your hair, and doing all sorts of time-wasting, inefficient activities.

While you're caught up in the busyness of the day, you don't mind these things; they're necessary breaks to alleviate stress. But on video, they're painful to watch. And the tape will clearly show that you can easily cut down on wasted time at least 10 percent without getting stressed.

How can you spend your time more efficiently? An article in *Money Making Opportunities* magazine (August, 1997) offers the following tips for increasing the efficiency of your daily routine:

- *Create blocks of prime time when you can concentrate on your hardest tasks without interruption.* Let everyone around you know that that during these certain hours you are completely unavailable.

- *Schedule easy tasks outside of this prime-time block.* Writing notes, reading trade journals, filing, and administrative chores can all be done at times when you're not completely focused on a project.

- *Keep your prime-time block sacred.* If your prime time is 2 p.m. until 4 p.m. don't even think about scheduling a dentist appointment at 3:00. This would break up your block.

> Evaluate the value of each task. Is all this work necessary? Or are you meeting some arbitrary standards that could be bent? You might take a close look at some tasks you thought were necessary and end up eliminating them. Or if someone else thinks these tasks are necessary, let that person do them.

Add 10% more productive hours to your day

You can't literally cram a 25th hour into a 24-hour day. But you can shift activities and priorities so more time is available for essential tasks.

Many people complain "There aren't enough hours in the day." But when you examine their days carefully, you find that there are more than enough hours to accomplish what they want. The problem is that they're frittering away those hours on nonessential tasks.

The biggest time-waster? TV...no question. A recent Roper poll shows that in the average American household, the TV is on 50 hours a week. Much of that time is spent watching "what's ever on" rather than a specific interesting program. The proliferation in channel choices has fed this time-waster; couch potatoes can now sit for hours and "channel surf" with their remote control.

If you feel you need the relaxation that "vegging" in front of the TV provides, try the following instead. Sit in your same easy chair. Flip on the stereo or radio to music you like. Let the sound surround you. Have a refreshing beverage and maybe even a snack.

Set in front of you all the materials you want to read but never get to—circulars, direct mail, newspapers, books, consumer magazines, trade journals. Then read them for fun. Have a pen and scissors handy; if an item warrants more careful study or filing at the office, clip it and bring it to work with you the next day. Reserve this time for pleasurable reading only; read only what interests you. Do this and you will gain relaxation and pleasure similar to what you gain by watching TV without wasting the time.

Gain 10% more energy

In Chapter 8, I discuss ways to revitalize your mind and body so you have more energy to get your work done.

But before you implement a full program of energy-boosting activities, here are some things you can do to give yourself an incremental lift in energy while you're working:

🕐 *Drink cold water, juice, or other fluids throughout the day.* Medical experts recommend consuming six to eight glasses of water for a variety of health reasons. But drinking cold liquid also has an immediate, refreshing effect.

🕐 *Wash your face.* Another revitalizing effect of cold water is its feel on your skin. If you work at home or are lucky enough to have an executive bathroom with a shower, try a mid-day shower. If not, wash your hands and face when you feel yourself tiring. It has a nice wake-up effect.

🕐 *Go to bed an hour earlier.* Sleep has a restorative effect. If you're just sitting around at night, killing time, consider turning out the lights and going to bed. The extra sleep will pay dividends in increased energy the next morning.

🕐 *Eat breakfast.* Even something small. Personally, I'm not hungry in the morning and the thought of eating breakfast repulses me. But on those occasions when I need more energy in the morning, a light snack about an hour after I get into the office helps revitalize me. I can't eat when I get up, but waiting the hour enables me to consume the snack without digestive problems.

🕐 *Avoid big meals in the middle of the day.* They make you sleepy. "Grazing" is the practice of breaking your food intake into many small increments rather than the traditional two to three big daily meals; some experts think it's healthier. A study in Prague found that people who consumed their daily caloric intake in more than two meals had fewer heart problems. Dr. David Jenkins of the University of Toronto speculates that grazing could mimic the effect that dietary fiber has in helping the body absorb nutrients. In a group of test subjects who consumed their daily caloric intake in 17 small snacks, cholesterol levels dropped substantially (www.nserc.ca, Web site of the Natural Sciences and Engineering Council of Canada).

🕐 *Don't drink alcohol during the workday.* Alcohol may make you drowsy and impair your mental abilities. At business lunches, order club soda with lemon or iced tea instead of wine or a cocktail.

🕐 *Take a multivitamin.* Many people are "into" vitamins, minerals, and health foods today, and perhaps you could benefit from such a regimen. But even if you don't have time to investigate nutrition, at least take a multivitamin. That way, your basic minimum daily requirements will be taken care of.

🕐 *Take a cat-nap.* If your work situation permits it and you feel the need, try a 15- to 20-minute nap when you're really tired. This can be especially effective if you don't get enough sleep at night. Keep the nap brief; longer than 20 minutes or so will leave you groggy for the rest of the day. Don't nap too late in the day; it can make falling asleep at bedtime more difficult (*Self* magazine, November 1995).

🕐 *Exercise.* Ashamed, I admit I am one of the millions of Americans who do not exercise. My wife used to be in that group too. But since she started walking and exercising, she looks and feels better and has more energy. Follow her example, not mine. Start a moderate exercise program right away.

Get out of bed 10% earlier

Don't oversleep. It wastes time and can make you groggy. In addition, if your biorhythm is such that morning is your high-energy period, sleeping late wastes the majority of your most productive time of the day.

How do you know when you are oversleeping? If you wake up naturally—that is, without an alarm clock—and you go back to bed, you're oversleeping. If you use an alarm clock and feel refreshed when you get up...but then fall back into bed cause it's warm, dark, and comfy...you're probably oversleeping.

Want a simple, proven way to boost your personal productivity? Get up and go to work an hour earlier every day.

Rather than making you tired, this one-hour early start is an incredible luxury. You can get coffee, check your e-mail, read the paper, catch up on correspondence, or review yesterday's work—in peace and calm—before the office gets frantic.

Waste 10% less time

By now you may think I am obsessed with personal productivity. You're right. I particularly hate wasting time. Therefore, I dedicate myself to eliminating time-wasting activities from my life. Do I recommend the same for you? Yes. Time is a limited resource. Once an hour is gone, you can never get it back.

Here is a list of some major time-wasters and how you might eliminate them:

1. *Mowing the lawn.* A high school kid could do this for $10 for you. Why waste the hour or let the summer heat sap your valuable energy?

2. *Raking your leaves.* Same as above. If you rake because you enjoy being outdoors in autumn, at least wear a Sony Walkman and listen to a book or seminar on tape.

3. *Shopping.* I rarely go to the mall, preferring instead to sit home and conveniently order products I need from mail order catalogs and Web sites. If you haven't yet tried e-commerce, I recommend it highly.

4. *Gift giving.* I especially like mail-order shopping during the holiday season. Sitting at my desk with catalogs and Web sites at my fingertips, I can get all of my holiday shopping completed in less than an hour. Best of all, once I order, I'm done. The catalog houses and Internet sites gift-wrap my items for me, enclose a card, and deliver them right to each recipient's door. No more midnight runs to the drug store for more ribbons and bows!

5. *Personal errands.* Running personal errands is a waste of your time. Consider hiring a personal assistant or using one of the many personal services firms that will do this stuff for you. There are people who will do your shopping, prepare your meals, walk your dog, water your plants,

even take your clothes to the dry cleaners—for extremely modest fees. Why not try them? Their dollar rate is almost always well below the dollar value of your time. So you gain, not lose.

6. *Cooking.* Shop at today's fantastic value-added super-markets. You can pick up a wide variety of prepared meals and other value-added foods (for example, cut and washed lettuce and chicken breasts seasoned and ready for the broiler) that reduce food preparation time virtually to zero.

7. *Housecleaning.* Why every busy businessperson with the income to afford a cleaning service doesn't hire one is be-yond me. Housework is pure drudgery and, for most of us, not the best use of our time. Not only does using a profes-sional eliminate this time-waster, but the employees of the cleaning service will go about the task more energetically and enthusiastically than you do—precisely because that's their job!

8. *Home repair.* Another major waste of time. Don't do it un-less you enjoy it. You can spend countless hours tracking down problems—a leaky roof, knocking pipe, weak-flushing toilet, odd noise in the attic—that trained profes-sionals can diagnose in minutes. Take advantage of their experience, pay their fee, and save your valuable time for more productive tasks.

9. *Community.* Only participate in groups—PTO, neighbor-hood watch, coaching kids sports teams, church, volun-teer fire department—if you believe in their worth and are personally enthusiastic. The more enthusiastic you are, the more you'll put into a group activity—and the more you and the group (or their cause) will gain from your par-ticipation. Don't join simply because you feel obligated to do so. Don't go through the motions and sit through the meetings without being a proactive participant—or even a leader—in the group. That only wastes your time...and theirs.

10. *Tax preparation.* The tax laws are so complex today, it's a mistake not to hire a CPA or other professional to prepare your taxes if you're earning $40,000 a year or more. Yes, some accountants charge a hefty hourly fee. But they can

do in a day what it would take you a week to accomplish. So even if the hourly rate is equal to or greater than the dollar value of your time, you'll still save. And often, the amount of the refund they calculate for you more than pays the cost of their services.

Think 10% faster

Thought impulses in the brain are transmitted as electrical signals between neurons. Electricity travels near the speed of light. So thought is nearly instantaneous.

Or at least, it should be. But watch people around you. Many are stumped by the simplest questions and can't make even the tiniest decisions.

What's the problem? It isn't that these people are stupid. They just haven't been taught how to think. Thinking, like anything else, is a step-by-step process. It can be taught, learned, practiced, and developed.

The steps of the thinking process are very simple: Identify the problem, assemble all pertinent facts, gather general knowledge, look for combinations, sleep on it, use a checklist, get feedback, team up with others, and give new ideas a chance. Once you understand this process, you'll have an easier time making decisions, solving problems, and coming up with good ideas.

Here are the nine steps to better thinking in more detail:

1. Identify the problem. The first step in solving a problem is to know what the problem is. But many of us forge ahead without knowing what it is we are trying to accomplish. Moral: Don't apply a solution before you have taken the time to accurately define the problem.

2. Assemble pertinent facts. In crime stories, detectives spend most of their time looking for clues. They cannot solve a case with clever thinking alone; they must have the facts. You, too, must have the facts before you can solve a problem or make an informed decision.

Professionals in every field know the importance of gathering specific facts. A scientist planning an experiment checks the abstracts to see what similar experiments have been performed. An author writing a book collects everything he or she can on the subject: newspaper clippings, photos, official records, transcripts of interviews, diaries, magazine articles, and so on. A consultant may spend weeks or months digging around a company before coming up with a solution to a major problem.

Keep an organized file of the background material you collect on a project. Review the file before you begin to formulate your solution. If you are a competent keyboarder, rekey your research notes and materials into your computer. This step increases your familiarity with the background information and can give you a fresh perspective on the problem. Also, when you type notes, you condense a mound of material into a few neat pages that show all the facts at a glance.

3. Gather general knowledge. General knowledge has to do with the expertise you've developed in life and business, and includes your storehouse of information concerning life, events, people, science, technology, management, and the world at large.

In many manufacturing plants, for instance, it is the gray-haired supervisor, the 20-year veteran, whom the young engineers turn to when they have problems. These senior workers are able to solve so many problems so quickly not because they are brighter or better educated than others, but because in their years of company work they have seen those problems—or similar ones before.

You can't match the veteran's experience. But you can accelerate your own education by becoming a student in the many areas that relate to your job. Trade journals are the most valuable source of general business knowledge. Subscribe to the journals that relate to your field. Scan them all, and clip and save articles that contain information that may be useful to you. Organize your clipping files for easy access to articles by subject.

Read books in your field and start a reference library. Think back to that 20-year plant supervisor. If he writes a book on how to troubleshoot problems in a chemical plant, and you buy the book, you can learn in a day or so of reading what it took him 20 years to accumulate. Take some night school courses. Attend seminars, conferences, trade shows. Make friends with people in your field and exchange information, stories, ideas, case histories, technical tips.

Most of the successful professionals I know are compulsive information-collectors. You should be too.

4. Look for combinations. Someone once complained to me "There's nothing new in the world. It's all been done before." Maybe. But an idea doesn't have to be something completely new. Many ideas are simply a new combination of existing elements. By looking for combinations, for new relationships between old ideas, you can come up with a fresh approach.

The clock-radio, for example, was invented by someone who combined two existing technologies: the clock and the radio. Niels Bohr combined two separate ideas—Rutherford's model of the atom as a nucleus orbited by electrons and Planck's quantum theory—to create the modern conception of the atom.

Look for synergistic combinations. If you have two devices, and each performs a function you need, can you link them together to create a new invention?

5. Sleep on it. Putting the problem aside for a time can help you renew your idea-producing powers just when you think your creative well has run dry.

But don't resort to this method after only five minutes of puzzled thought. First, you have to gather all the information you can. Next, you need to go over the information again and again as you try to come up with that one big idea. Then you'll come to a point where you get bleary eyed and numb. This is the time to take a break, to put the problem aside, to sleep on it and let your unconscious mind take over. A solution may strike you as you sleep, shower, shave or walk in the park. But even if the answer doesn't appear, when you return to the problem after a break, you will find you can attack it with renewed vigor and a fresh perspective. I use this technique in my writing: I put aside what I have written and read it fresh the next day. Many times, the things that I thought were fine when I wrote them can be much improved at second glance.

6. Use checklists. Checklists can be used to stimulate creative thinking and as a starting point for new ideas. Many manufacturers, consultants, technical magazines, and trade associations publish checklists you can use in your own work. But the best checklists are those you create yourself because they are tailored to the problems that come up in your daily routine.

For example, Jill is a technical salesperson well versed in the technical features of her product, but she has trouble when it comes to closing a sale. She could overcome this weakness by making a checklist of typical customer objections and practicing how to answer them. The list of objections can be culled from sales calls made over the course of several weeks. Possible tactics for overcoming these objections can be garnered from fellow salespeople, from books on selling, and from trial-and-error efforts. Then, when faced with a tough customer, she doesn't have to "reinvent the wheel," but will be prepared for all the standard objections because of her familiarity with the checklist.

7. Get feedback. Sherlock Holmes was a brilliant detective. But even he needed to bounce ideas off Dr. Watson at times. As a writer, I think I know how to write an engaging piece of copy. But when I show a draft to my wife, she can always spot at least half a dozen ways to make it better.

Some people prefer to work alone. I'm one of them and maybe you are too. But if you don't work as part of a team, getting someone else's opinion of your work can help you focus your thinking and produce ideas you hadn't thought of.

Take the feedback for what it's worth. If you feel you are right, and the criticisms are off base, ignore them. But more often than not, feedback will provide useful information that can help you come up with the best, most profitable ideas. One good guide: If only one reviewer complains about a particular item, you can ignore it. But if all three reviewers make the same comment, they're probably on to something—and you should take a closer look.

Of course, if you ask others to "take a look at this report," you should be willing to do the same for them when they solicit your opinion. You'll find that reviewing the work of others is fun; it's easier to critique someone else's work than to create your own. And you'll be gratified by the improvements you think of—things that are obvious to you but would never have occurred to the other person.

8. Team up. Some people think more creatively when working in groups. But how large should the group be? My opinion is that two is the ideal team. Any more and you're in danger of ending up with a committee that spins its wheels and accomplishes nothing. The person you team up with should have skills and thought processes that balance and complement your own. For example, in advertising, copywriters (the word people) team up with art directors (the picture people).

In entrepreneurial firms, the idea person who started the company will often hire a professional manager from one of the Fortune 500 companies as the new venture grows; the entrepreneur knows how to make things happen, but the manager knows how to run a profitable, efficient corporation.

An engineer may invent a better microchip. But if she wants to make a fortune selling it, she might team up with someone who has a strong sales and marketing background.

9. Give new ideas a chance. Many business people, especially managerial types, develop their critical faculties more finely than their creative faculties. If creative engineers and inventors had listened to these people, we would not have personal computers, cars, airplanes, light bulbs, or electricity.

The creative process works in two stages. The first is the idea-producing stage, when ideas flow freely. The second is the critical or "editing" stage, where you hold each idea up to the cold light of day and see if it is practical.

Many of us make the mistake of mixing the stages together. During the idea-producing stage, we are too eager to criticize an idea as soon as it is presented. As a result, we shoot down ideas and make snap judgments when we should be encouraging the production of new ideas. And many good ideas are killed this way.

More on how to get your brain to think 10% faster

If you still feel slow-minded after deliberately applying these nine steps, you may be losing mental sharpness as a natural result of aging.

The brain is critically dependent upon blood flow and requires one-fourth of all the blood pumped by your heart. As you age, blood flow to the brain can diminish. When that happens, cells begin a breakdown process that eventually leads to their death.

This "brain decay" begins around age 35 and accelerates dramatically when you reach age 50. Your ability to perform daily mental tasks can decline by 30 to 50 percent—and sometimes even more—during your lifespan.

And if you're limiting your fat intake, you're even more likely to be short-changing your brain. As you age, your brain actually loses weight—a decline of about 2 percent every decade after about age 40 or 50! To thrive, your brain must be supplied with phospholipids, vital nutrients that are derived from fat. Fat-poor diets can drain the phospholipid supply to dangerously low levels.

> To keep your mind nimble, use it often. Do the crossword puzzle. Read a book. Surf the Internet. Go to museums. According to a report in *Science News* (March 6, 1999), the very act of learning may create a "neural efficiency" in the brain that makes it easier for individuals to think!

You can combat mental fatigue and decline with a physical and mental exercise regimen. Researchers at the University of Pennsylvania Medical Center believe a lifetime of brain exercise can help stave off Alzheimer's disease, as well as other degenerative brain disorders. And a researcher at the Salk

Institute of Biological Studies has found evidence in a study of mice that running creates extra brain cells (University of Pennsylvania Health System, www.med/upenn.edu/news).

Speed up your reading time 10% or more

As John Naisbitt points out in his best-selling book *Megatrends* (Warner Books, 1984), we are in the midst of a transition from an industrial society to an information society. Because of this "information explosion," the amount of reading we must do to keep up in our industry is growing almost daily.

In-baskets across the country are overflowing with journals, reports, papers, memos, faxes, and letters—more material than anyone could possibly hope to digest. Although it's tempting to dump that towering pile of mail into the wastebasket, this is not a practical solution to the challenge of staying informed and competitive in your job. A better idea is to develop a systematic method for dealing with the daily influx of mail.

The following tips can put you in control of information overload, instead of vice versa:

- Be selective in the number of magazines, newsletters, and trade journals you subscribe to or receive. Analyze which give you the best return on your reading time and cancel those that are borderline, repetitive, or offer irrelevant information.

- Figure out which sections of each publication are the most useful to you. After reading one or two issues of a journal, you can begin to develop a feel for which columns, sections, and features you should read in careful detail and which ones you should either skim or skip altogether.

- Use the magazine's table of contents to distinguish between useful and extraneous information. If you can't read the articles right away, clip or photocopy items of interest and put them in a folder or in-basket for future reading. This keeps your stack of "must-read material" whittled down to a manageable level.

⊕ Use waiting or travel time to catch up on office reading. Whether you are on the bus or train, in the air, waiting in bank lines, or even on hold on the telephone, these spare moments, normally wasted, can be put to good use by reading.

⊕ Set aside a specific time each day for reading. An hour is usually sufficient. Pick a time when your schedule is relatively quiet and you expect few interruptions. Lunchtime or early morning may be the best periods. Keeping distractions to a minimum helps improve concentration.

⊕ If possible, read demanding or crucial material when your energy level is at a high. Some people work best early in the morning, whereas others get more done at night. Figure out when your energy peaks occur during the day, and do your most demanding reading during those times.

⊕ When reading difficult material that requires retention, take notes. Writing down important points aids in comprehension and memorization.

⊕ Take breaks. Studies show that most people can maintain good concentration for about 50 minutes, after which they need a 10-minute break to absorb more information and prepare for further work. Forcing yourself to continue reading when you are mentally tired is ineffective and inefficient as you tend to reread the same material over and over, and at a slower pace.

⊕ Develop a filing system for saving information on relevant or interesting topics. Five to 10 manila folders will do the trick. For example, if you are an analytical chemist you might have folders labeled "gas chromatographs," "liquid chromatography," "u/v/visible spectrophotometers," "atomic absorption." This kind of system helps you capture valuable facts and puts them right at your fingertips.

🕐 Set up a system for passing along pertinent articles to others. Give your assistant the names and addresses of friends, co-workers, clients, and colleagues with whom you regularly correspond. When you want to pass along a pertinent clipping, simply tear out the article, attach a note saying, for example, "send to Terry Henderson," and have your assistant do the rest. (If you don't have an assistant, do it yourself!)

🕐 Before you sit down to read for content, make sure you have everything you need. You should have a pen, highlighter, scissors, and a note pad or index cards (if you're reading study material), and the complete text of the article.

🕐 When reading trade magazines, tear out the reader service card and keep the card and a pen in front of you as you scan the magazine. By doing so, you can quickly get more information about the products mentioned in an ad or article by circling the appropriate key number on the card.

🕐 Take a speed-reading course or buy a book that teaches you how to read faster. Although most people can benefit from an analysis of their reading habits, this especially applies if you are a slow reader. Do you subvocalize (say words to yourself as you read)? Do you read everything at the same speed? Speed-reading can teach you to lose bad habits and develop new, efficient ones through training and practice.

🕐 As a guideline, an efficient reading speed for many types of nontechnical materials is between 400 and 800 words per minute. Slower speeds of 150 to 250 words per minute are appropriate for technical material. You may want to improve your speed if you are reading below this level.

Increase efficiency. Make your hours more productive. Gain more energy. Sleep less. Waste less time. Think faster. Read faster. Do these things only 10 percent better and together they'll multiply the improvements in your life many times over.

Chapter 4

Mastering the Time Management See-Saw

"Time eventually humiliates us all."
—Robert X. Cringely, author of *Accidental Empires*
(HarperBusiness, 1996)

Time and workload never seem to get in synch. In fact, often the opposite is true. You've heard the old saying, "When it rains, it pours." When we're already too busy, even more work hits our in-basket. When we're slow, we can't get the phone to ring and our e-mail file is empty.

The natural tendency is to work hard and practice good time management during the busy times, then coast during the slow times. Don't do it! The key to maximizing productivity is to spend all periods—down and busy—productively.

First let's look at turning downtime into productive time. Then we'll discuss the opposite situation—freeing your time when you're overloaded. Finally, we'll end with some more ideas to help you boost personal productivity in both peak and lull periods.

Use downtime productively

Let's say you are not being fully challenged and don't have enough work to keep you busy during the week. The key to success is to make yourself productive during these empty hours so they are not wasted. The temptation is to call in sick, plop into bed for a nap, or watch television. Don't do it! Always consider working hours as working hours, and make a commitment to do work during them.

How can you spend these hours productively if you have very little to do? The answer is: time-fillers. These are activities that you don't do as normal parts of your routine, but you do when you have extra time on your hands. The important thing about a time-filler is that it either earns you extra income, enhances your professional growth in some way, or has some other productive goal. Its purpose is to avoid wasting spare time and instead to use it productively.

Here are time-fillers that you can use to turn your "dead time" into productive, profitable time:

Time-filler #1: *Do pro bono work.* Is there a favorite charitable cause that could use your managerial talents or entrepreneurial services? Perhaps a local animal shelter, senior citizens group, library fund-raising drive, or community theater. If your schedule is not filled to overflowing with work assignments, volunteer to contribute your services to a worthy cause for low pay or no pay. In addition to sharpening your skills and making you feel good about yourself, you will be helping others and making useful contacts with people who may be in a position to hire you or refer business to your firm.

Time-filler #2: *If you work for yourself and things are slow, take a part-time job.* A growing number of firms hire freelancers or temps on a part-time basis. The professional works, almost like an employee, in the agency's offices one or two days per week according to a regular schedule. Although the pay may not match your regular day rate, it can be quite good and it does give you another steady weekly paycheck. This type of activity eliminates the angst that comes from being without work, and instead of having to find enough business to fill five days a week, now you only have to fill only three or four days. Try it!

Time-filler #3: *Teach.* In the 1980s, I taught adult education evening classes in writing at New York University as well as several other adult education programs. Although the pay is meager, it's a nice credential to add to your resume.

Teaching a class offers a number of other advantages. First, some workers who spend most of their time at the computer are often too solitary for their own good. One programmer told me, "I like programming but I don't get to interact with any people in this job." Teaching gets you into the world, out among people.

Second, teaching gives you exposure and enhances your reputation. (I have gotten several clients who called me after seeing my course described in the New York University course catalog.)

Third, you learn a lot about a subject by preparing to teach a course in it.

And fourth, the material gathered for a course can be recycled into an article, book, report, audiotape, lecture, and so forth.

If you want to teach, write to college, university, and high school adult education programs in your area and request their night school/continuing education catalog. Then write to the program director proposing a course on a topic that would fit in with their current program but which they do not now offer. This is how I got my teaching assignment at New York University.

Time-filler #4: *Learn a new piece of software.* Every time you master a new piece of software, you enhance your productivity for years to come and substantially increase your efficiency and overall profits. Yet most of us are usually too busy to take time out to learn new software.

So when you have a slow period, take advantage of that extra time to boost your computer skills. Some of the software you should be looking into includes: databases (for maintaining client lists), word processing (if you are not already using it, you should be), telecommunications (learn how to use that modem!), on-line information services (becoming familiar with one or two of these can save hours of research time), spell-checkers, spreadsheets, graphics, desktop publishing, and accounting.

Time-filler #5: *Clean out your files.* Not busy today? Okay. Go out, get some cardboard boxes or large plastic bags. Now go through your files and your office and throw away all the old files, papers, books, back-issues of unread magazines, and other junk cluttering your space—the junk we all save but don't need.

Reason to do this: Most of us, whether we work at home or in an outside office, have limited space. And you will soon fill up that space if you don't periodically purge yourself of the jetsam of life.

Time-filler #6: *Organize your office.* I know mine needs it! Too many notes and papers are pinned to my bulletin board and I never seem to have enough shelf space. Use your spare time to neaten and organize your clutter, or physically change or add to your office to make it more efficient.

I paid a contractor more than $12,000 to finish two rooms in my basement so I could use them for storing books, papers, and files that are old and no longer fit in my primary office. And you can never go wrong buying an extra four-drawer file cabinet or big bookcase to neaten the overflow of books and papers when your office gets too crowded.

Making your workspace better always pays off in increased efficiency. Even if you have only a couple of spare hours, you can always clean out and reorganize a desk drawer or two, right?

Time-filler #7: *Spend more time on each project.* Let's say you could normally handle four projects per month, but this month you only have one. One good way to productively use the extra time is by doing a better-than-usual job on the project you do have. You'll enjoy having the time to do a truly thorough job, which will reward you with a happy boss or client, as well as more assignments. So if project "B" and job "C" haven't come through yet, dedicate yourself to job "A" and it will pay off in the long run.

Time-filler #8: *Read.* One of my greatest frustrations is that there is so much to learn, so much to read, and never enough time to read it.

My wife and I frequently comment to each other that we could easily spend the entire day reading the material that crosses our desks, leaving no time for client work. But, since the clients come first, the reading is pushed aside for later or often neglected altogether. Sometimes I am truly saddened by all the good articles and books I want to read and that deserve to be read but that I will never have time to read.

Slow times should never be wasted in idle daydreaming; they are an ideal period for self-education. Read books, articles, and papers on whatever topics you deal with regularly in your work. For the successful person, education does not end with school, but is a life-long process. Oh, if only there were more hours in the day!

Time-filler #9: *Take a course.* Slow times are also good times to take a course in any subject that interests you or would add to your professional growth. Although the tendency is to take only business and computer courses, don't forget to treat yourself to something that's purely fun and appealing to your self-interest, such as short story writing, oil painting, Greek history, and so forth.

Time-filler # 10: *Be social with colleagues.* I seldom attend association or professional society activities because I simply don't have the time. But this type of networking is worthwhile. It can stimulate your thinking, expose you to new ideas, broaden your network of contacts, and even result in referrals and new business. So if you can fit it in, join a local chapter of a professional or trade group and go to the meetings. Get to know fellow specialists in your area. Once they get to know you, your phone may start ringing more frequently that it does now.

Time-filler #11: *Do something nice for yourself.* I remember when I quit my job in 1982 and began my freelance writing practice, I promised myself that the first thing I would do is take a week off and spend it doing fun things in Manhattan. Like many New Yorkers, I spent so much time working in the city that I never really got to see it as a tourist.

So if you have some extra time on your hands, do something nice for yourself. My desire now is to spend a month in a log cabin at a lake banging out a novel on a laptop PC. Now if only I can find the time...

Time-filler #12: *Become an expert in a specific field.* All of us work in areas about which we have some degree of knowledge (even though that knowledge may be only what we learned on the job). Wouldn't it be nice to learn about one or more of these disciplines in more detail? Wouldn't you contribute more and get noticed in a more favorable light?

When you have the extra time, go to the library and do some reading and research. Build a good clipping file of information. Build a small library of books on the topic. Spend spare time becoming an expert in a field; then sell this expertise as part of the package you offer clients or employees in that field. It will pay off.

Learn to handle pressure and juggle projects

Are you too busy? If you've been in the corporate world for a spell, you know how difficult it can be to cope with an overload of work. Here are some suggestions for doing so.

Learn to say no. It's scary to turn down work or say no to a manager above you. But when you're truly too busy, it's sometimes the best thing to do. After all, if you take on more than you can handle and miss a deadline or do shoddy work in order to make the deadline, that will do far more harm to your relationship and reputation than saying no.

I rarely say no to current clients, unless the deadline is so tight that I cannot possibly make it. If that's the case, I ask if there's any reason why the deadline can't be a few days longer, and I usually get it. (Many deadlines are artificial and have no logic behind them.) If they cannot be flexible, I politely explain that the deadline is too short, thank them for the offer of the job, apologize for not being able to take it on, and suggest they give it to one of their other resources (freelancers, in-house staff, ad agency, production studio).

However, I frequently say no to new prospects who call me during a busy period. When they start to describe their project or ask about my service, I stop them and say, "I'd be delighted to talk with you about this project. But I don't want to waste your time, so I must tell you now that I am booked through the end of September [or whenever]. If the project is not a rush or if you can delay it until then, I'd be happy to work with you. If not, I'll have to pass."

Amazingly, the usual reaction is not anger or hostility (although a few callers get mad); instead, most are impressed, even amazed. ("You mean you are booked through September? Boy, you must be good!" one caller said today.) In fact, turning down work because you are booked frequently creates the immediate impression that you are in-demand and thus tops in your field, creating an even stronger desire to work with you. Many people you turn down will call you back at the time you specify and ask, almost reverently, always respectfully, "You said call back in September. I have a project. Can you work with me now?" Try it. It works!

Busy people learn how to say no. According to Marilyn Machlowitz, the author of *Workaholics* (New American Library, 1980), management consultant Peter Drucker responded to requests for his time with a pre-printed card that read as follows:

Mr. Peter Drucker greatly appreciates your kind interest but is unable to: contribute articles or forewords; comment on manuscripts or books; take part in panels and symposia; join committees or boards of any kind; answer questionnaires; give interviews; and appear on radio and television.

Set the parameters. An alternative to turning down work cold is to set the schedule and deadline according to your convenience, not theirs. "Well, I am booked fairly solidly," you tell the prospect. "I can squeeze you in; however, it will take seven weeks [or whatever] instead of the usual three to complete your project, because of my schedule. If you can wait this long, I'll be happy to help you. If not, I will have to pass on the assignment."

Again, many prospects will turn to someone who can accommodate their original deadline. However, many others will say "yes" to your request and hire you on your terms.

Get up an hour earlier. I find that mornings are my most productive time. I work best from 7 a.m., when I usually start, to 1 or 2 p.m.; after that, I slow down. If I am extremely busy, I try to start at 6 a.m. instead of 7 a.m. and find that I get an amazing amount of work done during that first extra hour. Also, it makes me less panicky for the rest of the day because I have accomplished so much so early.

Work an hour later or work one or two hours in the evenings after dinner. If you usually knock off at 5 p.m., go to 6 p.m. Or, if you generally watch television from 8 p.m. to 10 p.m., work an extra hour and a half from 10 p.m. to 11:30 p.m. I prefer the extra morning hour for client projects; evening time is reserved for my own self-sponsored projects, such as books, articles, or self-publishing.

Put in half a day Saturday morning or Saturday afternoon. If you have to work weekends, Saturday morning—say, from 8 a.m. to noon—is the best time. You get that early morning energy and get the work out of the way so you can relax and enjoy the rest of the weekend. If you are not a morning person, try Saturday afternoon. If you put the work off until Sunday, you'll probably just spend all Saturday worrying about it or feeling guilty about it, so don't. Get it done first thing and then forget about it.

Hire a temp. If you are under a crunch consider getting temporary help for such tasks as proofreading, editing, research, typing, data entry, trips to the post office, and library research. Spend the money to get rid of unnecessary administrative burdens and free yourself to concentrate on the important tasks in front of you.

Break complex tasks into smaller, bite-size segments. Rush jobs are intimidating. If you have two weeks to work a major brochure, but put it off until the last three or four days, the task looms large and panic can set in.

The solution is to break the project into subprojects, assign a certain amount of the task to each day remaining, and then write this down on a sheet of paper and post on the wall or bulletin board in front of your desk.

Ask for more time. When you are just starting out, you naturally want to please co-workers and thus you agree to any deadline they suggest. In fact, you encourage tight deadlines because you believe that doing the work fast is a sign of doing your job right.

As you get older and more experienced, you learn two important truths. First, that many deadlines are artificial and can be comfortably extended with no negative effect on the client's needs whatsoever. And second, that it's more important to take the time to do the job right then to try and impress a naive client or supervisor by doing it fast. What matters, for example, is not that the software was coded fast but that it works, meets user requirements, is reliable, and doesn't have bugs. So if you need extra time, ask for it. This is real service to the client. Doing rush jobs is not.

Get a fax machine. Before the advent of the fax machine, if I had a project due Wednesday, I pretty much had to be done with it on Tuesday at 3 p.m. so it could be printed and ready for Federal Express pick-up by 5 p.m. Now with a fax machine, the job due Wednesday can be finished Wednesday at 4 p.m. and on the client's desk at 4:15 p.m.—giving me an extra day on every project.

Most corporate workers I know have fax machines. Some entrepreneurs don't. If your small business doesn't have one, get one. Don't waste time and money faxing documents at the local stationery store. Don't waste your time or other peoples' by making your fax compete with your modem and phone for use of one line; get separate lines for each. (Having the same number for phone and fax also is a sign to some people that you are not running a "real" business.)

Get e-mail. Learn to browse the World Wide Web and send e-mail over the Internet. You'll save time and energy and get more done. See chapter 5 for more information.

Stay seated. Georges Simenon, author of the popular *Inspector Maigret* series of mystery novels, wrote more than 500 books. How did he do it? Simenon said that he limited his writing vocabulary to 2,000 words so he would not have to use a dictionary (there are more than 800,000 words in the English language, with 60,000 new words added since 1966). This allowed him to work continuously, without having to stop, open, and search a dictionary for a word. The key to his success then, at least in part, was working without interruption—he kept going, and didn't let anything stop him while he was hot.

You've heard the term "seat of the pants" used to describe a method of working. Although it originally referred to a person who made decisions by instinct without a lot of planning or formal study, for office workers the definition is different: You apply the bottom of your pants (your rear end) to the seat (your chair), and stay there until the work gets done.

This means getting into your chair—and staying there. No using the VCR monitor in your office to watch TV. No quick trips to the cafeteria for a snack. No gossiping around the water cooler. This sounds trivial, but is in fact an important point. To get a lot of work done, workers must stay at their workstations. For office workers, the workstation is your desk and chair. Distractions are death to peak personal productivity. It's bad enough that many distractions—drop-in visitors, emergencies, telemarketing calls—already present themselves during a normal workday. Do not seek them out deliberately.

Don't commute—compute and telecommute. Commuting saps energy and wastes time. According to an article in *American Demographics* (January 1999), roughly 100 million Americans drive to work, with an average daily round-trip commute of about 70 minutes.

Despite the technology advances used by mobile workers (notebook PCs, wireless phones, pagers), commuting and other travel time is usually not as productive as desk time. Even if you carry a laptop, you can't use it standing at a bus station in the rain or when you're driving to work in your car.

One solution may be to arrange with your employer to telecommute part-time or full-time. When you telecommute, you work at home and are linked to your office electronically through one or more of the following: e-mail, the Internet, an intranet, local area network, fax, or phone.

Telecommuting offers several advantages. One, of course, is the elimination of your physical commute. Another is the increased personal productivity some workers experience being in the more isolated home environment versus the busy office.

In an interview with New York's *Daily News,* novelist Elizabeth Richards, who earned $1.4 million for the publishing and film rights to her first novel *Every Day,* says the best part of her job is "being able to work at home." Aside from the enjoyment, working at home or at an office near your home has the advantage of eliminating commuting, which can increase your productivity substantially.

According to the article *Telecommuting: The Convergence of Work, Home, and Family Spheres* (www.iamot.org) by Sara Pitman, studies show that telecommuting increases employee productivity by an average of 20 percent. The reason? Employees are happier, take fewer sick days, and are generally more motivated. And, since employees work out of their home, companies can reduce office space and costs.

Another time-saving advantage of working at home is the ability to eliminate the bother and trouble of buying, wearing, laundering, and dry cleaning business clothes. It also eliminates the time-consuming task of making yourself well-coifed each morning.

Ann Marie Harmony, president of In the Mood, a consulting firm, offers the following tips for making telecommuting work in her article "10 Success Secrets for Managing Telecommuters" (www.in-the-mood.com):

🕐 Install a separate phone line for business in addition to the regular home phone line. Always answer the business line in a business manner. Do not have a personal recorded message answer the business line. Not only is it unprofessional, but your callers may think they have reached a wrong number.

🕐 Regularly schedule 30-minute weekly teleconferences with your colleagues. Make it an automatic and predictable event: same day and time, same location. That way, people don't have to think about it—it's assumed that it's coming.

🕐 Equip yourself with reliable computer hardware and a fast Internet Service Provider (ISP) offering high quality service. Slow network speeds make telecommuting inefficient and costly.

🕐 Offer co-workers several alternatives for reaching you: phone, e-mail, pager, wireless phone. Let people know which of these is the best way to reach you when the need is urgent.

And what if you can't telecommute on certain days—or ever? Here are a few ways to make the time you use in your commute more productive:

🕐 If you drive, equip your car with a wireless phone. This way, you can conduct business during your commute. *Warning:* Pull over when you use your cell phone. Studies show an alarming number of traffic accidents involve people talking on their cell phones while operating their vehicle.

🕐 Listen to audio cassettes on business topics while you commute. Turn travel time into learning time.

🕐 Carry a portable cassette player with you to dictate correspondence.

🕐 Use a laptop computer to get work done while traveling in planes and trains. Make sure your laptop has a modem for connecting to your office network.

🕐 Carry at least two project files with you. Work on them while sitting in airports, standing on line, or during other "down time."

🕐 Always have a pad and pen with you to jot down ideas and thoughts.

Too busy? Count your blessings

One difficulty in managing time is caused by the fact that we rarely have just the "right amount" of work to do. Most office workers feel that they either don't have enough work or, if they are busy, have too much work and are overloaded.

People have a misconception about being busy versus not being busy. They think that if you are not busy, they don't expend much effort and therefore have lots of leftover energy. While if they are busy, they come home exhausted from doing all that work.

Actually, the opposite is true. If you are not busy, time drags, the day seems endless, and you drift through work in a malaise. Think back and remember the last time you were stuck in a boring class in college or high school, had to go to church or synagogue when you didn't feel like it, or had to listen to a boring speech, lecture, or conversation. You would look at your watch and it would say 10 a.m. You'd drift off, look at your watch an hour later, and it said 10:01 a.m.!

An hour hadn't even passed but when you are bored, the minutes seemed like hours! Being bored drains you, de-energizes you and not having enough work to fill one's day can be terribly demoralizing. In his novel *Even the Wicked* (William Morrow & Company), Lawrence Block tells the story of a low-level criminal, Benny the Suitcase, whose only job is to start mobster Tony Furillo's car in the morning:

> You turned the key in the ignition and when nothing happened you went back home and watched cartoons. Benny did this for a couple of months and then quit. "Nothing ever happens," he complained. Of course if anything ever did happen you'd have to pick him up with a sponge, but all he knew was the boredom was too much for him.

Being too busy is the better alternative. Although this may physically tire you, mentally it can make you feel happy, fulfilled, even energized. At the beginning of the day, plunge into your tasks, knowing that you are a productive individual with plenty of projects to attend to. At the end of the day, turn off your PC, put your feet up, and reflect on your success. Be happy that you achieved much during the day, yet still have a full schedule of important and fulfilling work ahead of you.

Chapter 5

Using Technology to Save Time

"The day is short, and the work is great."
—*Talmud*, "Ethics of the Fathers"

Unless you're a hermit living in a cave, you already know that technology has revolutionized the modern world, including the working pace of the business world. This chapter gives you a quick nuts-and-bolts discussion on equipment you must have—and equipment you should have—to maximize the hours you put in to get the job done every day. It covers recommendations on Internet connections, online services, computers, modems, CD ROM drives, fax machines, telephone systems, photocopiers, scanners, and voice-mail systems. Also included are my recommendations on software for word processing, desktop publishing, spreadsheets, graphics, virus protection, accounting, and contact management.

Ever since the typewriter was commercially introduced in 1873, advances in communication technology have enormously increased the speed and efficiency with which paperwork can be processed. Then the first word processor was introduced in

1965. It consisted of a magnetic-tape storage system linked to an electric IBM typewriter. The first personal computers were introduced in France in 1973.

Many people who are Baby Boomers or older resist technology, especially those of us who grew up pounding on IBM Selectrics or having a secretary type all our correspondence. But the fact is, technology can dramatically save you time and increase your productivity. The more you embrace it, the more you'll get done.

Choose a computer that's best for you

Do you need a personal computer ("PC" for short)? In today's workplace—yes. Get the best computer system and software money can buy. If you can't afford to buy, lease; the low monthly payments make computers affordable and you can lease software as well as hardware. Ask the computer reseller to recommend a system configuration in terms of processor, memory, and hard disk storage. Then get twice that—or at least as much above the recommendation as you can afford.

Reason? Whatever you buy today will cease being state of the art as soon as you learn to use it, so you can never have too much computer. For example, when I got my new system, I was thrilled to be buying "top of the line"—a 486 machine. The instant it was delivered, I read about the Pentium chip in the newspaper and realized I was already a generation behind. Now I hear talk about a P6 chip that will soon render the Pentium obsolete!

As of this writing, the top of the line personal computer for business desktop usage is a Pentium II chip operating at 233 to 300 MHz or higher.

According to the *Daily News* (April 30, 1997), the U.S. market for PCs expanded 13.6 percent in 1996, and the worldwide PC market is expected to show double digit annual growth for the rest of the decade. By the year 2000, Dataquest expects worldwide PC shipments to reach more than 131.7 million units for revenues of $264.3 billion. By the year 2001, more than 282 million PCs will be connected to the Internet.

"Not to be at least semi-computer literate today, or to keep putting off acknowledging that computers are the money-making tool of the century, is to keep your head in the sand while the rest of the world passes you by," writes Sheldon Schwartz in *Spare Time Opportunities* magazine (June, 1996).

Today, as PCs proliferate, more and more businesspeople are learning to keyboard—which is a good thing: It increases productivity and prevents miscommunication. For instance, bad handwriting costs U.S. businesses about $200 million a year, according to Zaner-Bloser, a handwriting textbook publisher (New York's *Daily News*, February 24, 1998).

Equip your computer system with as many productivity-boosting and time-saving tools as possible. Hardware should include:

- High-speed fax/modem (56 kbps or ISDN).
- Floppy disk drive.
- 1 GB Jaz drive.
- 6.4 GB or more hard-disk storage.
- 16X CD-ROM drive.
- PS/2 keyboard.
- 3-button mouse.
- Windows 98 or higher.
- 2 MB PCI video card.
- Tape backup.
- Laser printer.

As for software, here's what you'll probably want to consider:

- Word processing with spell-checker (Word or WordPerfect).
- Spreadsheet (Lotus, Excel).
- Contact manager or personal information manager (Act, Telemagic, InfoSelect).

- ◷ Presentation program (PowerPoint).

- ◷ Desktop publishing (Publisher 98, Adobe InDesign, Quark Xpress).

- ◷ Anti-virus (MacAfee, Norton).

- ◷ Accounting (Quicken, QuickBooks Pro).

Other productivity-boosting equipment

- ◷ *Scanner.* Scanners save time transforming hard copy research material into editable PC files you can incorporate directly into your document without rekeying. The Hewlett Packard ScanJet 3P scanner or an equivalent machine is perfect for the small office. The cost without options like feed trays is less than $500.

- ◷ *Photocopier.* You can get a decent small-office copier new for around $1,000 to $1,500. Home copier models, acceptable for office use, are available for under $700. I have had a Toshiba BD3110 for years and am still very satisfied.

- ◷ *Fax machine.* Fax machines and e-mail have replaced interoffice mail and the post office as the standard methods of transmitting documents. Get a plain paper fax—laser or ink jet. Avoid faxes that use thermal paper because this paper is difficult to handle and store and faxes printed on it fade over time. Buy the highest-speed fax you can afford. In 1996, I bought a new HP Fax 700 for around $600 and am very satisfied. It's an ink-jet machine and the copy qualities are excellent.

- ◷ *Modem.* Modems are inexpensive, so invest in the fastest modem the computer store can sell you—which of this writing is either a 56 Kbps or an ISDN modem. Slower modems take longer, increase your phone bill, and waste your time. An article posted on the *PC World* Web site (www.pcworld.com, February, 1997) reports that five minutes out of every hour spent on the Web is spent waiting for pages to load.

Communicate on-line

An article in *Men's Health* magazine (February, 1998) reports that almost three out of ten executives rank e-mail as their preferred form of business communication. An article in *Small Business Computing & Communications* magazine (March, 1998) notes that between one-quarter and one-third of all computer users use e-mail in order to avoid face-to-face communication with their bosses, co-workers, relatives, and friends. There is no doubt that e-mail is becoming a preferred mode of correspondence today.

But be wary about forsaking all human contact because you find e-mail easier and more productive. An OfficeTeam survey of 150 executives showed that 44 percent prefer face-to-face business meetings to other forms of communication, while only 34 percent prefer to do most of their business interaction via e-mail (*Continental*, October, 1997). "People like to talk," writes Peter Keen in *ComputerWorld* (January 11, 1999). "Voice is the main medium of human exchange." As evidence, Keen notes that cell phone usage hit the 10 million-user mark faster than either PCs or the Internet.

> You can use e-mail when you hook up with a service provider. A large number of white-collar professionals I know use CompuServe, America Online, or a direct connection via a local service provider to the Internet. CompuServe's toll-free number is 800-848-8990. America Online is 800-827-6364. (Although America Online bought CompuServe in 1997, the two continue to function as separate services.)

In addition to speeding research, being online will save you time corresponding with colleagues, co-workers, vendors, and customers. Instead of having to print and mail a manuscript or transfer files to a floppy disk, you simply hit a button and instantly download your copy to your recipient's e-mail address. According to an article called "5-Minute Mail" in *Wealth Building*

(March, 1998), e-mail reaches its destination within five minutes, 87 percent of the time.

Before you hook up to the Net, however, be aware that being online can also rob you of precious time. Frivolous e-mail correspondence, online chat rooms, and idle Web surfing are all huge time wasters. The Internet is an efficient tool for those whose intention is to work more productively, but too often it serves as a time-wasting alternative to doing real work. As a medium, it has powerful potential, but the quality of content sometimes falls short. Writer Orson Scott Card says, "We converse with a lot more people via the Internet only to discover that most of them are talkative idiots." (*CIO* magazine April 15, 1998).

Once you start using e-mail, you'll become dependent on it to get your work done. That's why round-the-clock availability of Internet access is so important to me. Markus Allen, President of MailShop USA, a PA-based lettershop, advises having more than one Internet connection. I use an ISP as the primary and AOL as secondary.

Controlling your e-mail volume

PC World gives the following tips for reducing your e-mail traffic to a reasonable level:

1. *Read the subject header first.* This will help you decide if you should open the message at all. Don't waste your time reading unnecessary e-mail messages.

2. *Be selective about giving out your e-mail address.* To reduce the load of unwanted e-mail, give your address only to special clients, colleagues, co-workers, and others who really need it.

3. *Use just one mailbox.* If you have multiple e-mail addresses with different services, give out only one of them to co-workers and business correspondents. And find one e-mail front end that will handle them all. Possibilities include Microsoft Office 97's Outlook, Eudora Pro, and Windows 95's bundled e-mail program, called either Microsoft Exchange or Windows Messaging, depending on the version.

4. *Stop spam.* When you receive unsolicited junk mail (called spam), check the bottom of the sales pitch for an "autoresponder" address. Send an e-mail message to the address with the word "remove" in the subject area. This should remove your address from the mailing list. If it does not, find out whether your service provider has a customer service department that will deal with spammers. A squeaky wheel gets less garbage.

5. *Prevent needless responses.* Let your correspondents know when they don't need to respond. Make sure you haven't invited a response when you don't want one.

> Writing in *Network Magazine* (January, 1999), Devine Wolfe advises businesses to develop a written e-mail policy and train employees in its usage. "Make it clear that e-mail is taken just as seriously as other forms of office communication," says Wolfe, who notes that the contents of e-mail messages can constitute grounds for discrimination, harassment, and other forms of corporate misconduct.

Increase telephone productivity

Today, for under $200, you can buy a business telephone with a wealth of built-in productivity-enhancing features. The ones you should consider are as follows:

- *Push button dialing.* Rotary phones are obsolete. If you have one, get rid of it. You are wasting too much time dialing. And rotary phones can't navigate through the menus of many of your prospects' voice-mail systems.

- *An LED display.* This is used to display the status of various features and functions. When you have Caller ID (see below), the display can identify the source of incoming calls. Some regional telephone companies offer Caller ID that shows you the name of the caller or their company as well as the phone number. You can decide whether to take the call, have call forwarding, or voice mail handle it. This is a great time-saver.

Caller ID is especially valuable for screening calls. You can use this feature to isolate yourself from interruptions during time set aside for other tasks. It is also useful for help desks, support lines, customer service departments, and other departments who can respond more professionally when they know in advance who is calling. Calling number ID can work with call-forwarding, call-waiting, and three-way calling.

🕐 *Memory dial.* You can store important phone numbers in memory and dial them at the push of one button. This can significantly cut down dialing time when calling your most important prospects and customers.

🕐 *ISDN compatibility.* ISDN, short for Integrated Services Digital Network, is an internationally accepted standard for high-speed data communication. ISDN lines transmit data at higher rates than regular telephone lines. You'll save time and reduce phone bills when communicating with customers by modem, e-mail, online services, fax, and the Internet.

🕐 *ISDN line.* To take advantage of ISDN technology, you will need an ISDN phone line, as well as an ISDN phone. The main advantage of ISDN is much faster Internet access, especially to sites with heavy graphics. As I write this, Bell Atlantic tells me they will charge me $37 a month to convert one of my phone lines to ISDN, plus a 2 cents a minute transaction charge. You can get a pretty fancy phone with built-in ISDN capability for under $150.

🕐 *Multiple lines.* Your customers should never get a busy signal when they call you. A solution to this problem is to have more than one phone line. You can get a phone that can handle two different phone lines (with two different numbers even) for under $150. You'll probably want separate lines anyway for your phone, fax, and modem.

🕐 *Conference calling.* Use the conference calling feature (called "three-way calling" by some telephone companies) to call multiple parties and link them in a conference call.

🕐 *Redial.* When you get a busy signal or have another problem when dialing, just hit the redial button. The phone will automatically redial the number for you, saving you time and effort.

🕐 *Hold button.* Avoid using your hold button. You should not put prospects on hold, especially if you called them. A better alternative is to have incoming calls routed to another phone or to a voice mailbox.

🕐 *Extra function keys.* Get a phone with some extra function keys, so there are some keys that do nothing. This allows you to add new services and features as they become available without upgrading or replacing your existing telephone equipment.

🕐 *Extra length cord.* If you like to get up, stretch your legs, and walk around while you talk on the phone, get an extra long phone cord—at least six feet. A short cord, if bent and twisted, may also cause a crackling or interruption on the phone line.

🕐 *Headset.* The advantage of this feature is that it leaves your hands completely free to make notes, pull files, and use your computer while you talk.

🕐 *Speakerphones.* Use the speakerphone only when you need to have a group of people participate in a call. Don't use your speakerphone for regular one-on-one calls; the voice quality is inferior to a regular phone handset.

🕐 *Voice mail.* For a nominal charge, you can get voice mail provided by your local telephone carrier. Rather than have a telephone answering machine take your calls, messages go into a voice-mail system in the phone company's central office; you retrieve messages using a special code. Voice mail eliminates the need to maintain and occasionally replace an answering machine. Unlike phone answering machines, voice mail keeps working even when the power goes off, preventing missed calls.

I have set up my telephone so that when I am on a call and another call comes in, it is routed directly to the voice mail. This way, the caller I am speaking with is not interrupted by an annoying call-waiting signal.

◔ *Voice-activated dialing.* Speech recognition enables callers to 1) dial numbers by saying the number, 2) dial specific parties by speaking the person's name, and 3) automatically identify themselves to the network by voice without having to remember or punch in a personal identification number. This saves time when dialing and eliminates the need to carry an ID card or address book.

◔ *Message waiting indicator.* Users are automatically alerted when they have messages waiting for them in voice mail. Notification can take place via a message on the phone's LED display or an audible tone. This eliminated the time wasted calling in to find out if there are any messages.

◔ *Single number reach.* If you have different telephone numbers—several business phones, a cellular phone, and a home phone—callers can reach you by calling a single number. This eliminates the need for callers to remember multiple numbers when they want to track you down.

◔ *Call transfer.* Allows you to transfer calls to other people within your office. Use it to transfer calls meant for others in your company, eliminating the need to ask the caller to call back.

◔ *Do not disturb.* You can set your phone to automatically route calls to another phone (such as your assistant or secretary) or to your voice mailbox if you want to work undisturbed.

○ *Selective call acceptance.* A variation of Do Not Disturb, this feature allows certain calls to get through your Do Not Disturb screen, based on the caller's phone number or ID. Therefore you can avoid calls you do not want to get while enabling important prospects, colleagues, and family members to reach you at all times.

○ *Voice mail retrieval.* Lets you retrieve your voice-mail messages from phones other than your own. Useful for those who sometimes attend meetings outside of the office.

○ *Call forwarding.* Call forwarding means the phone forwards (sends) the call to another phone. You can have calls forwarded immediately when the caller receives a busy signal or when the phone rings but is not answered.

○ *Call waiting.* Allows a single phone on one phone line to simultaneously receive multiple calls. When the user is on the phone and another party dials that number, she hears a beep tone. The tone lets her know that someone else is calling. The user can ignore the call and let the phone ring (or combine call waiting with another service to have the second call picked up and answered by voice mail). Or, by pressing a key, she can put the first call on hold and take the second call. The user can toggle back and forth between the two calls at will.

The features that are available in your area code depend on your particular phone company. Call them for details.

Using the phone efficiently and effectively

The telephone has a great deal of power, yet as a basic business instrument it is often misused. The first contact many people have with you is over the phone. They probably will form a lasting impression of you on the basis of that conversation. Fortunately, with a little tact and attention to what you say and how you say it, you can use the phone as an effective tool in getting and keeping cooperation, sales, and goodwill.

🕐 *Promptness counts.* Answer your calls on the first or second ring, if possible. This gives the caller the impression that you are responsive and efficient. Occasionally, you may have to delay answering a call to finish an urgent task or because you were momentarily away from your desk. But no office phone should ring more than four times before being picked up by someone. Otherwise, you may risk losing a valuable call.

🕐 *Identify yourself to the caller.* When you answer, identify yourself. A "hello" is not sufficient; give your name and department. By saying "Mike Bugalowski, Quality Control," you give callers the information they need, and you also prompt them to identify themselves in return. This also shows that you are businesslike and ready to be of service.

Apply this rule even when picking up the phone for someone else. Say, "Tod Pitlow's office, Mike Bugalowski speaking," so callers will know someone is taking responsibility for helping them.

🕐 *Avoid offensive screening questions.* When screening calls, avoid using phrases that seem to challenge callers or imply that they may not be worth talking to. For example, the screening phrase, "Do I know you?" is offensive because it puts callers in the embarrassing position of having to guess whether you remember them and it implies that you may not be interested in speaking to callers unknown to you.

When you answer the phone for someone else, there are certain screening phrases you should also avoid. These include: "Will she know where you're from?" (I don't know; I'm not a mind reader.) "And what is this in reference to?" (Do you want the long version or the short version?) "What company are you with?" (Does he only talk with people from companies?) "And you're from...?" (Kentucky, originally.) "And what does this concern?" (His wife's gambling debt.)

🕐 *Tell callers to whom they are being transferred.* People don't like to get the runaround. So if you need to transfer someone, first explain why and where you are switching the call. It is also wise to give the caller the extension or the number of his or her party, in case the call gets disconnected.

🕐 *Cover yourself.* Leaving a phone unattended is a sure-fire way to lose important calls and irritate those trying to reach you. We've all had the frustrating experience of calling a business and letting the phone ring 10 or 15 times with no answer. When that happens, we get angry and think, "What a poorly run company they must be to let the phone ring so long."

If your phone is not hooked to voice mail or an answering machine and if there is no one available in your office to answer your calls while you are away, have the calls transferred to a receptionist or someone else who agrees to cover for you. Be sure to tell that person where you are going, when you will be back, and any telephone number where you can be reached. Then collect your messages and return your calls promptly.

🕐 *Take complete messages.* When you take a message, listen carefully and write down everything. Get the person's name, telephone number, affiliation, and the name of the person or department the caller is trying to reach. Even when callers are in a rush, don't be afraid to ask them to repeat spellings, pronunciations, and numbers if you didn't hear clearly the first time. Taking complete, accurate messages avoids confusion and ensures that calls can be returned promptly.

🕐 *Putting people on hold.* No one likes to be put on hold. But if it's necessary, first explain why you need to leave the line, how long you'll be gone, and then ask if the caller can hold. Wait for a reply; no one likes being put on hold before they have a chance to object. When you ask, you'll find that most people say "okay" and appreciate your courtesy. When you return to the phone, thank the caller by name for waiting.

Make sure the caller isn't on hold for more than a minute. If you need to be away from the phone longer than that, ask if the caller would prefer that you call back. Promise to call back at a specific time and do so.

🕐 *Be pleasant.* Everyone has a bad day now and then, but it's not smart to show it in person or on the phone. Anger, impatience, or boredom can come through a phone line quite clearly and make a caller defensive or nervous. If you are unpleasant or brusque on the phone, people may go out of their way to avoid dealing with you.

So no matter what your mood, strive to be pleasant and alert throughout a conversation. When people call at a bad time, ask if you can call them back and propose a specific time.

A good rule to remember is to treat callers the way you would treat guests in your office or home. You'll win their respect and goodwill. Courtesy and attentiveness will help you succeed through improved public image, better customer relationships, and increased sales.

🕐 *Keep it short.* Brief conversations save time and your listener will be grateful for them. Everyone enjoys a certain degree of personal conversation, such as "How are you?" or "How was your trip?" but lengthy personal discourses or general ramblings on are inappropriate, and probably boring to most people.

It's a good idea, therefore, to stick to the point and to be prepared when you are planning or expecting a call. I suggest you write down the major points you want to cover on a sheet of paper. When you talk, look at the sheet and check off each point as it is discussed. This technique will help you keep on the subject and help you avoid getting sidetracked. If an unexpected subject comes up and you need to obtain additional information, explain this to the caller and make arrangements to call back with the answers.

Invest in wireless communication

Years ago, carrying a cell phone may have been viewed by some cynics as a status symbol in a culture that admittedly seems to worship "busyness." Countless movies and TV shows used cellular phones to portray characters obsessed with work and unconcerned with the rest of life.

Today, wireless communications is less about impressing people and more about enhancing the user's ability to communicate with anyone they want, at any time, no matter where they are located—an essential component of using time wisely and remaining competitive into the year 2000 and beyond. According to the Cellular Telecommunications Industry Association (CTIA), there are 47 million wireless users in North America, with that number growing by 30 percent a year (*Fortune*, December, 1996).

Downsizing has had an unexpected consequence. It has extended business hours so that workers never know where or at what time they'll need to call a customer, colleague, supervisor, or prospect. Professionals in global markets especially have to be able to take and make calls at odd hours outside the office. In fact, almost 40 percent of today's workers consider themselves "mobile," and seven out of 10 of all U.S. professionals spend more than 20 percent of their time away from their desks. According to *InfoWorld*'s "1995 Remote Access Study," almost one in three corporate employees surveyed uses some type of remote access technology to keep in touch with clients and colleagues when away from his or her desk. In addition, the number of individuals working at home had grown to 46 million in 1995 (*Fortune*, December, 1996). It is now well-established that by enabling more workers to be mobile or telecommute, wireless technology can significantly lower facilities costs while increasing worker productivity.

There's no doubt that the communications requirements of the work force today are different than they were a decade ago. Wireless technology, considered a luxury at one time, is now as essential a tool to many businesspeople as their fax machine, beeper, modem, and PC.

There are two basic types of wireless phone systems: cellular and Personal Communications Service, or PCS. On one level, the difference is the frequency at which the systems operate. Cellular—from which we get the term "cell phone"—operates at frequencies of 800 to 900 MHz and is the older, more established technology.

PCS is a newer, lower-powered technology. Competitive to cellular, PCS operates in the 1.5 to 1.8 MHz range. Manufacturers promoting PCS say the phones and air time cost less, while the lower power consumption allows longer phone operation before replacing or recharging batteries.

While the industry offers a number of wireless technologies that are both complementary and competing, its current obsession with standards is designed to make sure everything works with everything else—seamlessly. Stringent standards mean no lost calls, no failed dials, no loss of voice quality, as well as dialing methods that remain consistent from region to region. Choosing the right wireless service will save you both time and money. An article printed in New York's *Daily News* (January 29, 1999) offers the following advice for choosing the best wireless service:

🕐 Consider your calling patterns. For frequent travelers, a one-rate anytime, anywhere plan may be your best bet. But, if you are one of the 80 percent of wireless subscribers who don't use your mobile phone outside your calling area, a local plan probably makes more sense.

🕐 Consider when you make most of your phone calls. Pick a plan where the airtime charges are least during your most busy calling periods.

🕐 Consider only the services you need. Resist the temptation to sign up for every new service because they're neat and nifty.

Before you run out and buy any new, high-tech equipment, keep in mind that you're probably using only a small fraction of the capabilities in your current systems. Take a "technology day" where you do nothing but explore the power and capabilities you already have in the equipment you currently own. Probably there's a lot of time-saving technology there, yours for the using as soon as you master it.

Chapter 6

Delegation and Outsourcing

"Getting results through people is a skill that cannot be learned in the classroom."
—J. Paul Getty, American business executive

As I discussed in the introduction, you are a limited resource. Even if you could somehow be productive every minute of your life, there are still only 24 hours in a day. And you can't add a 25th. Or can you? Not to your own day, you can't. But you can get 25 or 50 or 75 hours worth of work done in a single day—or much more—by delegating or outsourcing some of your work to others. In fact, delegating or outsourcing is the only way to do this.

Practice the art of delegation

In his book *Time Power* (Harper & Row, 1987), Charles R. Hobbs defines delegation as "the act of controlling through others." Delegation, then, is more than just giving work to people; it's managing those people so they get that work done correctly and efficiently. Here are some suggestions that will help you be a more effective delegator/manager:

- ○ *Demand solutions, not problems.* Hobbs' key delegation principle is for managers to require employees to bring them solutions, not problems. Example: An assistant once began to give me a lengthy explanation of why we could not open certain files e-mailed by a client and the various ways in which we might try to resolve the problem. I interrupted and said, "I trust you. I just want the files in electronic or hard copy form. Don't tell me the details; I don't care." Get your people to focus on your ends and they'll find the means.

- ○ *Use "what-if" logic.* My sister Fern is a manager at a trade association. When employees bother her with questions or problems she feels they can answer on their own, she asks them, "If I were dead, what would you do?" Says Fern, "Nine times out of 10 they figure it out on their own without my help or further involvement."

- ○ *Target productive work times.* Managers who think their assistants will diligently attend to tasks handed to them at 3 p.m. on the Friday before a 3-day weekend are fooling themselves. Assign involved tasks to employees when they are most likely to produce results. Fifty-one percent of 150 executives surveyed by Accountemps said Tuesday is the day of the week when employees are by far the most productive, reports the article "Dream Week For Bosses: Every Day is a Tuesday" (*The Record*, May 4, 1998). The worst day for productivity? Friday.

- ○ *Add a human touch.* The most valuable qualities you can develop within yourself are patience, kindness, and consideration for other people. Although machines and chemicals don't care whether you scream and curse at them, people do.

Your staff and co-workers are not just engineers, scientists, administrators, clerks, and programmers; they're *people,* first and foremost. They are people with families and friends, likes and dislikes. People with feelings. Respect them as people and you'll get their respect and loyalty in return. But treat them coldly and impersonally and they will lose motivation to perform for you.

Corny as it sounds, the Golden Rule—"Do unto others as you would have others do unto you"—is a sound, proven management principle. The next time you're about to discipline a worker or voice your displeasure, ask yourself, "Would I like to be spoken to the way I'm thinking of speaking to him or her?" Give people the same kindness and consideration that you would want to receive if you were in their place.

Don't be overly critical. As a manager, it's part of your job to keep your people on the right track. And that involves pointing out errors and telling them where they've gone wrong.

But some managers are overly critical. They're not happy unless they are criticizing. They rarely accomplish much or take on anything new themselves, but they are only too happy to tell others where they went wrong, why they're doing it incorrectly, and why they could do the job better. This takes up a lot of time in exchange for very little results.

Don't be this type of person. Chances are, you have more knowledge and experience in your field than a good many of the people you supervise. But that's why the company made you the boss! Your job is to guide and teach these people—not to yell or nit-pick or show them how dumb they are compared to you.

Let them fail. Of course, to encourage people, you've got to let them make some mistakes.

Does this shock you? I'm not surprised. Most workers expect to be punished for every mistake. Most managers think it's a "black eye" on their record when an employee goofs.

But successful managers know that the best way for their people to learn and grow is through experience and that means taking chances and making errors.

Give your people the chance to try new skills or tasks without a supervisor looking over their shoulders—but only on smaller, less crucial projects. That way, mistakes won't hurt the company and can quickly and easily be corrected. On major projects, where performance is critical, you'll want to give as much supervision as is needed to ensure successful completion of the task.

And what happens if an employee or subcontractor screws up really badly? "It ain't as bad you think it is," says Colin Powell. "It will look better in the morning. Get mad, then get over it." (*Leadership,* March 9, 1999.)

Be available. Have you ever been enthusiastic about a project, only to find yourself stuck, unable to continue, while you waited for someone higher up to check your work before giving the go ahead for the next phase?

Few things dampen employee motivation and slow things down more than management inattention. As a manager, you have a million things to worry about besides the report sitting in your mailbox waiting for your approval. But to the person who wrote that report, each day's delay causes frustration, anger, worry, and insecurity.

So although you've got a lot to do, give your first attention to approving, reviewing, and okaying projects in progress. If employees stop by to ask a question or discuss a project, invite them to sit down for a few minutes. If you're pressed for time, set up an appointment for later on that day and keep it. This will let your people know you are genuinely interested in them. And that's something they'll really appreciate.

Improve the work environment. People are most productive when they have the right tools and work in pleasant, comfortable surroundings.

Be aware that you may not be the best judge of what your employees need to do their jobs effectively. Even if you've done the job yourself, someone else may work best with a different set of tools, or in a different setup, because each person is different.

If your people complain about work conditions, listen. These complaints are usually not made for selfish reasons but stem from each worker's desire to do the best job possible. And by providing the right equipment or workspace, you can achieve enormous increases in output...often with a minimal investment.

Show interest in their lives. You can benefit by showing a little personal interest in your people: their problems, family life, health, and hobbies. This doesn't have to be insincere or over-done. It can simply be the type of routine conversation that should naturally pass between people who work closely.

Have you been ignoring your employees? Get into the habit of taking a few minutes every week (or every day) to say "hello" and chat for a minute or two. If an employee has a personal problem affecting his mood or performance, try to find out what it is and how you might help. Send a card or small gift on important occasions and holidays, such as a 10th anniversary with the firm or a birthday. Often, it is the little things we do for people (such as letting workers with long commutes leave early on a snowy day, or springing for dinner when overtime is required) that determine their loyalty to you.

Be open to ideas. You may think the sign of a good manager is to have a department where everybody is busy at work on their assigned tasks. But if your people are merely "doing their jobs," they're only working at about half their potential. A truly productive department is one in which every employee is actively thinking of better, more efficient methods of working—ways in which to produce a higher-quality product, in less time, at lower cost.

To get this kind of innovation from your people, you have to be receptive to new ideas; what's more, you have to encourage your people to produce new ideas. Incentives are one way to motivate employees to be more productive. You can offer a cash bonus, time off, or a gift. But a more potent form of motivation is simply the employee's knowledge that management does listen to him or her, and does put employee suggestions and ideas to work.

When you listen to new ideas, be open-minded. Don't shoot down a suggestion before you've heard it in full. Many of us are too quick, too eager, to show off our own experience and knowledge and say that something won't work because "we've tried it before" or "we don't do it that way." Well, maybe you did try it before, but that doesn't mean it won't work now. And having done things a certain way in the past doesn't mean you've necessarily been doing them the best way. A good manager is open-minded and receptive to new ideas.

Give your people room to advance. If a worker doesn't have a place to go, a position to aspire to, a promotion to work toward, then the position is a dead-end job. And dead-end workers are usually bored, unhappy, and unproductive.

Organize your department so that everyone has opportunity for advancement, so that there is a logical progression up the ladder in terms of title, responsibility, status, and pay. If this isn't possible because your department is too small, perhaps that progression must inevitably lead to jobs outside the department. If so, don't hold people back; instead, encourage them to aim for these goals so that they will put forth their best efforts during all the years they are with you.

Delegate whatever you can. "Many things can be delegated to people who will not do them the way you would, won't do them as perfectly as you would, but will wind up with the same result," writes Dan Kennedy in *No B.S. Time Management for Entrepreneurs* (Self Counsel Press). "Every one of these things should be delegated."

> Giving others work makes them more engaged in their jobs and saves you time. In her book *Workaholics,* Marilyn Machlowitz quotes psychotherapist Maryanne Vandervelde: "If you never have to cook your own dinner, take your own shirts to the laundry, arrange social engagements, worry about the details of a move, or stay home with a sick child, you can work harder, longer, and more efficiently."

Professionals who delegate are basically selling their time to an employer or a client, yet many office workers fritter their valuable time away handling the most mundane tasks. A better strategy is having employees or subcontractors do noncritical tasks for you.

Reward productive behavior. As management consultant Michael LeBouf notes, "The things that get rewarded get done." If you want people to get more done, create incentives for them to do that. One of the most popular incentives is "comp days"—

days off given in return for extraordinary efforts during crunch periods.

The art of delegating is one that improves with practice. The more often you let other people help you get work done, the more often you'll see the positive results. You will have more time to do the things that only you can do, and you'll be getting much more than 24-hours worth of work done each and every day.

Get with it—outsource

"All well and good for the corporate manager," some of you are now saying, "but I don't have employees, so I can't delegate."

Wrong. We all delegate every day. Every one of us. For example, instead of pressing our own pants, we tell the dry cleaner to do it. Instead of cleaning up the kids' toys, we tell the kids to tidy up after themselves.

Those who don't have employees still delegate. But we delegate to vendors: service firms, freelancers, independent professionals, independent contractors, and others who will do what we tell them, for a fee rather than a salary. The practice of delegating work to vendors instead of staff employees is called *outsourcing,* and its popularity has grown tremendously in recent years.

A Coopers & Lybrand press release (January 24, 1996) reports a survey that shows that in 1996, 81 percent of America's fastest-growing companies hired temporary, part-time, or contract employees. In 1996, NASA outsourced operation of the space shuttle to a consortium of private contractors (*Daily News*, October 1, 1996). And Dun & Bradstreet Information Services reports that 40 percent of small businesses outsource at least one function (February 4, 1996).

One factor contributing to the growth of outsourcing is ongoing corporate downsizing. From 1980 to 1993, the Fortune 500 companies eliminated 4.4 million jobs, downsizing a quarter of their work force (*Power Freelancing*, Mid-List Press, 1995).

In addition, more and more Americans are becoming self-employed. These include writers as well as the word processors, clerks, programmers, graphic designers, and other professional and clerical services necessary to support them. *Occupational Outlook Quarterly* estimates that more than 15 million workers are self-employed, with 3 million owning their own incorporated businesses.

An article in *The Record* (August 10, 1997) reports that the use of part-time workers is growing. Part-timers made up 16 percent of the national work force two decades ago; today they are 18.5 percent of workers—22 million people—according to the Bureau of Labor Statistics.

> Manpower, the world's biggest staffing agency, now employs 1.5 million people. According to the National Association of Temporary and Staffing Services (NATSS) 21 percent of temp workers in the U.S. can be classified as "professional and technical."

Why don't some companies outsource more? Some people hesitate for the following reasons:

- They think they're too small to need help.
- They don't have enough work to keep an assistant busy.
- They don't make enough money to be able to afford to pay someone else to do some of their work.

But as you become busier, you realize the amount of work you can do (and therefore the amount of income you can generate) is limited by your own energy and the number of hours you can work in a day. One way around this is to spend more of your time on billable work, especially work that earns a high hourly rate. To do this, you have to free up some time by not doing work that is not billable or work that is billed at a low rate. This is where hiring outside help comes in.

You make money by thinking and producing. Everything else—learning how to use a particular computer program, scanning source materials, going to the library, buying supplies—is a waste of time that could be spent on productive work. Some or all of these nonessential activities can easily be outsourced to others.

What should you outsource? Businesspeople outsource all different kinds of tasks including:

- Research.
- Filing.
- Typing and word processing.
- Mailing list and database management.
- Telephone selling and telemarketing.
- Customer service.
- Proofreading.
- Sales and marketing.
- Bookkeeping and accounting.
- Computer programming.

You can outsource all of these or some of these tasks. It's up to you. My policy is to do all the high-end work myself and outsource the administrative, clerical, and secretarial work to subcontractors (which I'll discuss in a minute).

Obviously, to make a profit, you have to pay the subcontractor less money than it would cost you to do the work yourself. This means either the subcontractors charge less per hour for their services than you do—or they charge less for the task because, given their high degree of proficiency, they can do it in a much shorter time frame than you can.

For example, I don't do my own filing, since I can pay someone to do it for me. It costs a fraction of the money I'd make spending the time on my writing and consulting projects. My attorney is more expensive and earns fees equivalent to mine, but I still use him on contracts and for other needs. Not only does he do a much better job than I would, but he can do in one hour (and bill me for one hour) what would take me half a day or more.

Outsourcing versus adding staff

Let's say you are interested in getting more help around your office. A major decision is whether to hire an employee or an outsource.

When you hire employees, they generally work on your premises using your office space, equipment, and supplies. You pay them a salary and often provide benefits such as sick days, vacation, and health insurance.

When you outsource, you contract with an individual or small firm that provides the services you need on a fee basis. This fee can be a project fee but is usually an hourly fee. Independent contractors typically work on their premises, using their office space, equipment, and supplies. You pay their invoice like you would pay a bill for any product or service you buy.

I have had both staff employees and subcontractors, and prefer the latter to the former by a wide margin. Here's why:

1. Subcontractors and other outsourced workers can perform as well as full-time employees but, on average, earn 40 percent less. Only 12 percent get a pension, and only 15 percent get health-care benefits. Therefore, they are cheaper to employ.

2. There is no long-term commitment and no recurring overhead. You pay subcontractors only when you give them work to do. Employees get paid as long as they show up, whether they have work to do or not. When you don't need subcontractors, they work for their other clients (or take time off), and you don't pay them.

3. Subcontractors are independent and responsible for their own welfare. Employees may depend on you for guidance, career satisfaction, and other needs—a responsibility you may not want to deal with.

4. Using subcontractors is less complex, from an accounting and paperwork point of view, than having employees. Employees require social security tax, FICA, worker's compensation, and other complexities. Independent contractors are paid as vendors. *Note:* The Internal Revenue

Service requires that people who are paid as independent contractors work on their premises and have other clients. Consult your accountant or tax attorney.

5. Subcontractors are more motivated because they are sellers and you are the buyer. They have a customer-service orientation which is a welcome change from the attitude of resentment or indifference many employees seem to have toward the boss.

6. Subcontractors provide their own equipment and office space, buy their own furniture, and pay their own utility bills. Often the subcontractor will have better equipment than you do, and as their client, you get the benefit of this equipment without buying it.

   Subcontracting can actually reduce your overhead and capital costs. Hiring employees increases it because you have to supply them with a fully equipped work space.

"Outsource everything other than your core function," recommends Stephen M. Polland in an article in *Dan Kennedy's No B.S. Marketing Letter* (December, 1998). His advice includes replacing full- and part-time staffers with independent contractors or other entrepreneurs, leasing or renting rather than owning hard assets, and focusing on personal productivity and profitability.

Where to find help through outsourcing

When my long-time staff secretary quit to take another job, I wondered where I would find another assistant. A colleague suggested that instead of hiring a full-time secretary, I could find a typing/word processing/secretarial service to handle my needs.

I looked in the local paper and yellow pages and called several services. I explained I was a busy writer looking for substantial secretarial support and asked each service—most of whom were individuals working from their homes—whether they would be interested in having a client who would provide them a substantial amount of business on a regular basis.

Every secretarial service I talked to was excited at the prospect of having such a client! Apparently, the word-processing and typing business is sporadic and project-oriented; having a regular client on retainer was unusual and a welcome change that would bring greater income and financial security.

I interviewed several word-processing services and chose one person. I explained that I would buy 30 hours of her time a week, by the week, and pay for a month's worth of service in advance at the beginning of each month. In return, I wanted the best rate she could offer me and a high level of service.

This person, who is now my assistant, works for me from her home in a town eight miles away. It's close enough that she can easily come over to do some work here or pick up materials if required, but most often we work by phone, fax, and e-mail. In fact, her small word-processing business has a part-time messenger to serve me and her other clients and I see her only a few times a year.

This "virtual office" approach has many advantages and few drawbacks. In addition to the advantages of outsourcing already discussed, I can work in privacy without having my assistant physically present (privacy and solitude are, to me, prime productivity boosters).

The only drawback is that my subcontractor isn't here all of the time to run certain errands, but I found a solution: I hired my former secretary as a second subcontractor. She works for me after her regular job, from 4:30 p.m. to 7:30 p.m. and can therefore go to the post office and bank and do other errands. I also have an independent sales rep who negotiates deals for me with corporate clients, a literary agent who does the same with publishers, an accountant who does my taxes, and a freelance bookkeeper who handles accounts payable and receivable. Obviously, I am a big fan of outsourcing. It works for me and I recommend that you try it.

I found my sales rep when I went to a trade show and attended a workshop on self-promotion for freelancers. I was so impressed that I called the presenter after the seminar and asked if she would represent me so that I could outsource all of my personal selling to her. She agreed and it has worked beautifully ever since. She is compensated similarly to the way literary agents are compensated, based on a percentage of my gross sales.

Start small. Hire a part-time secretary or word processor to work for you one day a week. If you can keep this person busy, and if you like having the help and feel it frees you to increase your output and income, you can always buy more of the person's time or, if he or she is too busy, hire a second helper.

One caveat: Since many of your colleagues may not use subcontractors, you may not be able to find someone through referral. Call people who advertise word processing, typing, or secretarial assistance in the local town paper and Yellow Pages. Meet with them face to face for an interview before hiring them. Start on a trial basis and don't promise anything more regular until both of you are satisfied the relationship is working well.

You might also consider using college students who can be hired as part-time assistants or summer interns. The problem is that after the summer, or when they graduate, they're gone. The value of an assistant increases as that person learns your procedures and business over time; this advantage does not exist when you hire college students and other transients who don't stick around. A professional word processor or secretary running his or her own service business, on the other hand, wants to make that business grow and is looking for long-term client relationships. That's why I prefer to outsource to professionals rather than to students.

The value of delegating and outsourcing

Look around you. Everywhere within a one-hour drive are co-workers, colleagues, suppliers, vendors, retailers, service firms, and other resources that are ready and willing to do the work you want to avoid. They'll iron your clothes, clean your apartment, even wash your hair for you!

My uncle Ira, a successful entrepreneur, taught me the lesson of valuing one's time and not wasting it on trivial tasks. When I moved from Baltimore to New York City to take a job, Ira asked me, "Are you eating balanced meals?"

No, I replied. I had a tiny kitchen and a pint-size refrigerator in my cramped Manhattan apartment. I ate pizza, subs, Chinese food, and other take-out. But my mother had promised to give me some recipes for healthy meals, which I intended to cook.

"Don't waste your time," said Uncle Ira wisely. "Go to the coffee shop or diner on your block. For five or six bucks plus tip, you'll get a meal including soup, salad, beverage, meat or chicken or turkey, potato, and vegetable. They'll cook it for you, service it to you, take away the dishes—and it will cost about the same as making it yourself."

While I still prefer to eat at home rather than in restaurants, I understood and began practicing the principle: Your time has value. Don't waste it. If you can buy a thing at less cost than the value of your time to do it yourself, buy it.

I agree with the philosophy of "make or buy" described by consultant Richard V. Benson in his book *Secrets of Successful Direct Mail* (NTC Business Books): "Make only that to which you bring a unique quality and buy everything else around the corner." I hope I bring a unique value to the books and copy I write for my publishers and clients. I know I don't bring it to a turkey dinner.

Polish up those people skills

We all know people with great "people skills" and sometimes wonder, "How do they do it?" It's simply a matter of knowing the basics of how to deal with other people and then making a conscious effort to put those basics into practice. Here are seven habits of businesspeople who know how to get the most out of the vendors they delegate or outsource to:

1. *They present their best selves to the public.* Your moods change but your vendors, customers, and colleagues don't care. Make a conscious effort to be your most positive, enthusiastic, helpful self, especially when that's not how you feel. If you need to vent, do it in private.
2. *They answer phone calls promptly.* Few things annoy people more than not having their phone calls returned. Get back to people within two hours. If you can't, have your voice mail guide them to others who can help. If you're really uncomfortable with certain people and don't want to talk with them on the phone, answer their query through a fax or e-mail. Or call when you know they won't be there and leave the a message on their voice mail.

3. *They call people by their names and ask questions about their lives.* Take the time to learn and use everyone's name, especially secretaries. Most people don't. You don't have to glad-hand everyone, but if you see a child's picture on someone's desk, they'd probably appreciate your asking, "How old is your daughter?" Establishing some common bond makes the other person more receptive to working with you.

4. *They meet people halfway.* Sometimes we're right and the other person is wrong, but many people I observe seem to enjoy going out of their way to rub this fact in the other person's face. Give instructions, corrections, and criticisms without making the other person feel stupid or ignorant, such as, "That's a good idea, but given the process variables, here's another approach we should also consider."

5. *They listen carefully before speaking.* A sure sign you are not listening to the other person is that you can't wait to say what you want to say. As soon as the other person pauses, you jump in and start talking. Even if you think you know how the story ends, listen to the other person. This person's knowledge and grasp of the situation may surprise you. If not, listening shows you considered his or her opinion and didn't just steamroll over the thought.

6. *They maintain eye contact.* When you're talking with someone, look him or her in the eye at points in the conversation. If you're explaining something while typing on a keyboard, take your eyes away from the screen now and then to look and talk directly at the other person.

7. *They are not afraid to admit when they are wrong.* People are afraid that other people will think they are incompetent if they admit to being wrong. The opposite is true. Andrew Lanyi, a stock market expert, explains, "The more you are willing to admit that you are not a guru, the more credibility you gain" (source: personal interview). No one knows everything, and everybody knows people make mistakes. If you refuse to admit your mistakes or if pretend to know everything, people won't trust you when you are right and do know the answer.

> Although they will never admit it, vendors have favorite and least-favorite clients. The rating you get as a client depends, in large part, on how well you treat the vendor as a business colleague and a human being. Despite claims that "every client is important," favorite clients often get preferential treatment; unpopular clients frequently go to the bottom of the priority list.

Poor communication is yet another barrier to working effectively with the people you delegate or outsource work to. Here are steps you can take to get your message across so everyone understands and no one is frustrated by the communication process:

1. *Listen and make sure you understand.* Listening is a skill that requires your full attention. Don't have a conversation while you're checking your e-mail or searching Web sites. Do one thing at a time and you will do each thing well.

2. *Prove you understand—feed it back.* When another person asks you a question or makes a statement, repeat it back in your own words and ask whether that's what the person meant. Very often, what he or she said—or what you heard—is not exactly what the person was trying to get across...and the two of you need to try again.

3. *Never underestimate the intelligence of the average person.* People who don't know your company, products, or technology may simply lack the technical background, data, and aptitude—and not intelligence. Explain technical concepts in plain, simple language. Avoid jargon or at least define technical terms before using them. A "fractional T1 circuit" may confuse your boss, client, or electrician but everyone understands the concept of a "telephone line."

4. *Talk to people at their level, not yours.* In addition to keeping things simple, focus on what's important to the other person, which is not necessarily what is important to you. For example, a graphic designer I know goes into elaborate explanations of kerning and fonts when all I want to know is whether to make the headline bigger.

5. *Make sure they get it.* People often don't ask questions for fear of being perceived as stupid. Encourage listeners to stop you and ask questions if they don't understand. Ask them questions so you know whether they got it. If not, find out what they don't understand. Then make it clear to them.

6. *Don't assume.* The old joke goes, "When you *assume*, you make an *'ass* of *u* and *me.'*" If you want someone to run a simulation on Windows 98, for example, make sure they have Windows 98 installed on their PC and know how to use it.

7. *Don't let your annoyance and impatience show.* Sure, it can be frustrating explaining what, to you, are familiar topics, especially to people who don't have the background. But if you act annoyed, lose your patience, or become arrogant, your listener will be turned off—and you'll make an enemy instead of an ally.

8. *Budget communications time into the schedule.* Part of the frustration people feel explaining projects, policies, and objectives is the time it takes, which they could be spending on their "real" work. The solution is to accept that communication is a mandatory requirement on every project and budget communications time into your schedule accordingly.

9. *Use the 80/20 rule.* The most effective communicators spend 80 percent of their time listening and only 20 percent talking. Many of us like to lecture, pontificate, or explain details of no interest to the other person. Instead, let the other people tell you what they need and want, then give it to them. When you waste a person's time, your relationship becomes less profitable—and they can quickly lose enthusiasm.

---

10. *Make a friend.* If there is chemistry or camaraderie between you and the vendor, let your relationship flow and grow naturally. You shouldn't force a connection where there is none, and you don't have to be a social butterfly when you're not. But as a rule, people prefer to deal with people they like. So make it easy for the other person to like you. Or at least don't give them reasons to dislike you.

Here are some additional tips to improve your ability to deal effectively with other people:

- *Prefer positive to negative statements.* Instead of "George didn't finish coding the system," say "George got 95 percent of the coding done." Instead of saying something is bad, say it's good but could be made even better. Instead of saying someone "failed" to do something, just say he didn't do it.

- *Don't speak when you're angry.* Cool off. Don't feel you have to answer a criticism or complaint on the spot. Instead say, "Let me give it some thought and get back to you...is tomorrow morning good?" This prevents you from saying things you'll regret later or making snap decisions.

- *Don't use value judgments to make people feel bad about mistakes.* Avoid the implication that errors in judgment, which are temporary and one-time, are due to character and intelligence flaws. Don't say "that was stupid"; instead say, "We can't ever let that happen again." Focus on preventing future repetitions of the mistake rather than assigning blame.

- *Be courteous but don't overdo humility.* Be pleasant and personable, but avoid fawning. Treat other people with respect and insist they do the same with you in return. For example, if a person is clearly technology-phobic, don't falsely flatter that person with malarkey about how quickly they're catching on...unless they really are.

🕐 *Empathize before stating an opinion.* Don't seek out an argument; argue only when necessary. And make the conversation collaborative rather than adversarial. Say, "I understand" when the other person gives his or her opinion. "I understand" doesn't mean you agree; it means you heard what that person said and considered it in forming your own opinion, which you're now going to present.

🕐 *Apologize completely.* Apologies should be unconditional: "I was wrong," not "I know I did X but that's because you did Y." Don't try to bring third parties or external factors into the equation. The bottom line is: It was your responsibility. Admit your mistakes and move on.

Use long-distance delegation and outsourcing

In today's global society, many of us deal with colleagues and suppliers who might be across the country or even around the world. We can still offload tasks to them, but managing the long-distance relationship has some added challenges, especially when different languages, cultures, and time zones are involved.

In an article in *Quality First* newsletter (February 25, 1991) business writer Marilyn Pincus gives the following five tips for working effectively with long-distance co-workers and vendors:

1. Distant co-workers are like customers. Do your best to serve them.

2. Try to personalize some of your conversations with distant co-workers. This helps establish a friendly environment. "When individuals feel kindly toward one another, there's a natural tendency to cooperate," says Pincus.

3. Listen carefully. Make sure everyone understands who is to do what and when.

4. Notify distant co-workers immediately of any delays or complications.

5. Identify expectations. For instance, if you're only available during normal business hours, distant workers may be required to take phone calls from you early in the morning or late at night, and possibly at home. Are they willing?

Do you feel you have to do everything yourself? Then you will never get everything done. Only by delegating or outsourcing to others can you go beyond your own limited personal effort and energy and make the most of every second of every day.

Chapter 7

Getting Organized

"Life is tough; it takes a lot of your time."
—Sean Morey, comedienne

If you don't think it's necessary to be organized in order to use time efficiently, think again. The average adult spends 16 hours a year searching for misplaced keys (*Reader's Digest,* September, 1998). An article in *Business Marketing* (March, 1997) reports that, according to an Internet survey of executives, being disorganized wastes at least an hour a day. At the end of a year, that's an awful lot of wasted time!

Getting organized does require effort, but the long-term rewards far exceed the short-term costs. People have asked me, "Doesn't it take a lot of time to go through all your to-do lists and systems each day?" I answer, "A lot less time than if I didn't have these systems and was less organized!"

On the other hand, the fear that time management technology may be too complex is well-founded. Some time management systems and products do take more time than they save.

The key is simplicity. My advice: Use what works for you and discard the rest. If a method is not comfortable, or a tool too complex, find something else.

> A 1995 study by the Merck Family Fund found that 62 percent of surveyed adults agreed with the statement, "I would like to simplify my life" (*The Record*, January 3, 1999). Yet most people don't make even the tiniest effort toward making their lives simpler. Even when they view not having enough time as the number-one or number-two problem in their lives, they spend zero time and effort seeking to remedy the situation. They continue their disorganized ways and refuse to change, which of course means the condition of not having enough time will not change either.

Get it together

"Organization is the key to moving forward in life or in business," says professional organizer Sandee Corshen (*American Way*, March 15, 1998). "You can't deal with today if yesterday is staring you in the face."

Disorganized people are inefficient, because they have to expend extra time and effort—calling the bank to get a duplicate copy of a statement already received and now lost, running to the crowded mall at the last minute to buy a forgotten holiday present, standing in line at the post office on April 14th waiting to mail income tax returns. All these activities waste time because of poor organizational and planning skills.

Here are some techniques that can help you organize your life and save time both at work and at home:

1. *Carry a pocket to-do list and a pen at all times. Write down thoughts and ideas as they occur.* Just as a computer's random access memory is erased when the power goes out, our brains lose track of thoughts, ideas, plans, and

tasks as we tire or take on too much new information. Carry a pad and pen so you can jot reminders, notes, ideas, and priority items as you think of them. It takes no work for the paper to remember them. But it exhausts your brain to do so. Why take the chance of having the day's priorities fade from your awareness? Write it down.

2. *Write down thoughts and ideas as soon as they occur.* The key to superior achievement is not having ideas—everyone has loads of them—but implementing them. You can't implement an idea if you don't remember it and make it an action item. You won't remember your ideas unless you write them down as soon as they occur. If you wait even an hour, you'll forget—and never record—more than 90 percent of the ideas you have.

    Again, most people don't have a shortage of ideas. But they do have too-short idea lists...because they don't write things down.

3. *Create filing systems for every aspect of your life.* To be truly well-organized, you have to create a specific place for all information and ideas. The best way to do this is to have a well-organized filing system covering every aspect of your life, not just major work projects. For instance, have you ever had an appliance break down that you thought might be covered by warranty, only to discover that you have no idea where the receipt and warranty are? The solution I use is to keep warranties, receipts, and instruction manuals for all household appliances and consumer electronics in a big three-ring binder labeled "HOME." Also included in the notebook are bills and guarantees for major home repairs, such as our new roof and added family room.

    The advantage of such a system is that I can quickly retrieve the papers I need without a time-consuming search. It also eliminates the problem of lost documents. With the document quickly in hand, we can easily and inexpensively take care of household problems either by troubleshooting them on our own (following the instructions we've saved) or by taking advantage of manufacturers' warranties that are still in force. This saves a considerable amount of time and money.

4. *Don't be a pack-rat.* Clutter is the enemy of efficiency. To reduce clutter, periodically, purge your file cabinets, hard disk drive, and bookshelves of old material you no longer need. Rule of thumb: If you haven't looked at it in a year or more you can probably throw it out. (Exception: Bank statements, income tax papers, and other financial records. These should be kept for seven years.)

5. *Keep a calendar of appointments and deadlines.* In Chapter 1 I stressed the advantages of posting to-do lists on a wall near you so they are always visible. "Out of sight, out of mind," is an old saying and a true one. If something isn't in front of your eyes, it tends to get tucked away in the back of your mind.

   Professionals with busy schedules and multiple tasks may want to use a more sophisticated system than my simple wall-mounted 8½ x 11 in. to-do lists. "Visual organizers" can solve the problem. A visual organizer is a wall-mounted system for prominent visual display of a continually updated calendar, schedule, task or to-do list. Most visual organizers are made of a piece of laminated plastic that can be mounted on a wall and written on with colored markers. The writing can be erased with a paper towel or eraser, making it easy to add updates and corrections to the schedule as needed.

6. *Cork a wall.* Bulletin boards are another tool that help you stay organized by putting tasks, papers, memos, lists, business cards, project schedules, policies, procedures, and other priority items in constant view.

   If you use a bulletin board but find you run out of space too easily, consider affixing cork panels to all or part of a wall in your office. The cork wall gives you a convenient, easy, highly visible system for organizing and displaying work materials.

   Cubicle workers often complain about being in cubicles, but one advantage of cubicles is that the walls are covered with soft material into which pushpins can easily be inserted. Therefore, if you're in a cubicle, every vertical surface can be used as a bulletin board.

7. *Keep a clean desk.* In the movie *How to Succeed in Business Without Really Trying,* Robert Morse convinces his boss that he is a hard worker by littering his desk with papers, coffee cups, and cigarettes to give the appearance of busyness. And it works—in the movie. But reality is something else: According to an article in *The Record* (January 18, 1999), the average executive loses six weeks a year retrieving misplaced information from messy desks and missing files.

   A messy desk is also an impediment to productivity. It limits your actual workspace because only a small fraction of the desk surface can be used for your current project; the rest is tied up as a storage medium. And you can't fully concentrate on the current task because the other papers staring in your face distract you by serving as a constant reminder of other pressures and work to be done.

8. *Put things in the same place every time.* I mentioned at the beginning of this chapter that the average adult spends 16 hours a year searching for lost keys. This won't happen if you put things in the same place every time. This organizational tip goes for In all aspects of your life...business projects, financial documents, pictures, momentos, keys, medical records, receipts, warranties, gloves, mittens, raincoats, boots, lunch boxes, tools. Keep each item in the same place all the time. If you get into this habit, remembering where things are becomes automatic and the items will always be there when you look. Until then, keep a master list of common items and their locations as a memory aid.

9. *Keep things in their appropriate space.* Clutter is the enemy of organization and productivity. Clutter occurs when materials, equipment, and tools for one task or area spill out into another area. Home-based workers frequently tell me that their home offices, intended to be confined to a spare bedroom or finished basement, have spilled out into other living areas such as the dining room or kitchen table.

   Put everything in its appropriate place. Use storage racks, stackable boxes, shelving, and whatever else helps you organize your possessions. Kids' toys stay in the toy box, newspapers for recycling stay in the pantry, and so on. If the pantry is full with papers, you have to take them to the recycling center and not let them spill into the kitchen.

Stop to take a pulse

Frank Bettger, in his best-selling book *How I Raised Myself From Failure to Success in Selling* (Prentice Hall, 1970), comments:

> One of the greatest satisfactions in life comes from getting things done and knowing you have done them to the best of your ability. If you are having trouble getting yourself organized, if you want to increase your ability to think, and do things in the order of their importance, remember there is only one way: Take more time to think and do things in the order of their importance.
>
> Set aside one day as a self-organization day, or a definite period each week. The whole secret of freedom from anxiety over not having enough time lies not in working more hours but in the proper *planning* of hours.

"I dedicate one afternoon or evening a week to doing nothing but relaxing at home," said technical writer Amy Shogan in an interview with *Intercom* magazine (February, 1999). "The catch is, while I 'relax' I tie up all the loose ends that we don't usually find time to do during the week." For Shogan, this includes sorting through mail, paying bills, returning calls, writing out a list of to-do's, reading, and planning for the following week. In the same article, Nancy Coleman, also a technical writer, advises drawing up the next day's to-do list at the end of each day. The list, says Nancy, should include the top three to five things that must be done immediately.

These strategies will all help you keep a finger on the pulse of your professional and personal life so you never have to waste time wandering around wondering what to do next.

Organize, store, and retrieve critical data

Irrelevant information is a great time waster, but relevant information that is not organized properly can also steal away precious hours of work time from a very busy schedule. Organizing information wisely increases its value to you; sloppy information organization decreases its utility.

The computer gives us an enormous advantage in managing information assets: Information converted to computer file format is much more easily manipulated, stored, retrieved, transmitted, and used than paper files.

If you are a professional working primarily with information, your computer files are perhaps your most valuable asset. Efficient use of them can save you time and effort while making you more productive. Poor computer file management can cause you to waste hours searching for data and recreating documents and images that already exist (but that you can't find).

Therefore, you should practice good digital-file management techniques. Digital files need to be organized in a sensible fashion and labeled in such a way that they can quickly and easily be retrieved, by a variety of selection criteria (key word, topic, project, customer, version, content, date) when needed.

In an interview with *Publishing & Production Executive* magazine (January, 1999), Neil O'Callaghan, vice president of Applied Graphics Technology in New York City, defines digital asset management as "a system and its associated workflow processes which facilitate the organization of digital media files—images, logos, graphics, pages, text, fonts, video, audio, and so forth—in such a manner as to allow for easy querying, asset information retrieval, asset identification, asset conversion, and export into a myriad of applications."

Even minor technology features can greatly enhance digital asset management. Two examples are Windows 95 and bookmarks. In DOS and Windows 3.1, computer files were limited to eight characters, resulting in all sorts of arcane file names in a creative effort to make them memorable and retrievable—which usually failed. Windows 95 and higher permit much longer file names, so file names can be more specific and descriptive, and thus easier to find and retrieve.

Another valuable tool is the bookmark feature included on most Web browsers. When you find a Web site you'll reference frequently or even occasionally, you can use the bookmark feature to add it to a list of favorite Web sites. These are stored in the browser for future reference, and are available whenever you access the Web. This prevents you from forgetting key Web site addresses and having to search for sites you've already visited.

> If you have a lot of files on a particular topic, project, or customer, maintain an index of them as a separate file. For instance, if the customer is General Motors, make all the files begin with GM; that way, they are all grouped together on your directory—without the need to create a subdirectory. The index file would be called "GMINDEX." In it would be a list of all file names, followed by a brief description. Therefore, "GMPR1" would be press release number one about the GM account.

Here are some tips for organizing your electronic files more efficiently:

- *Keep a set of "boilerplate" files.* These are pieces of text, graphics, drawings, routine correspondence, and presentations you've created for one job that you can reuse in other jobs. If you write sales proposals, for example, one boilerplate file might be your company's corporate bio that appears at the end of each proposal. If you write field inspection reports, much of the language might be similar or even exactly the same from one inspection to the next. Why reinvent the wheel each time? Name these files and keep a master list of them so you can find them easily when you need them.

- *Keep a directory that enables you to locate boilerplate documents quickly by topic.* It doesn't do any good to have a great boilerplate paragraph on disk when finding it takes more time than rewriting it from scratch.

- *Get a scanner.* Many times, you'll be incorporating into your own work sentences and paragraphs from other documents created by other people (being careful not to plagiarize, of course). You will have hard copies of these documents but not the electronic files. It's a waste of time to key these documents into your computer by hand. Scanning saves a lot of time. You can buy a decent scanner today for under $500.

☉ *Use logical filenames*—"JSMEM1," for example, for memo number one to John Smith, or "OUTREP1" for a report on outsourcing.

☉ *Always type the file name at the top of page one of the document*, as follows: "filename: OUTREP1." Often you come across a hard copy of something you've written in a file folder, and want to find the electronic file so you don't have to rekey it. Putting the name of every file on the first page of the document makes it easy to find the electronic files. If you can't, you have to scan or retype the material, which is boring as well as a waste of your time.

☉ *Store any document you might reuse in whole or in part on your hard drive.* Make sure your PC has at least several gigabytes of hard disk storage to accommodate a large number of stored documents. When evaluating whether to add a document to your collection, the rule of thumb is: When in doubt, don't throw it out.

Organize your paper overload

Not all the information you need will be stored on a computer. There will always be paper files that need to be organized in some recognizable manner before you find yourself squished into a corner of a room overflowing with boxes and file folders. According to Stephanie Denton, a professional organizer, the average U.S. executive spends the equivalent of six weeks a year searching for misplaced information (*Men's Health*, May, 1997). There's got to be a better way.

"Practice good filing 'hygiene,'" advises my colleague Jeff Davidson in an article in *Bottom Line/Business* (November, 1997). "Don't let papers pile up. File what you need and toss the rest. If information is available elsewhere, don't add it to your files."

101 Ways to Make Every Second Count

An article in the New Jersey *Record* (December 29, 1998) gives the following filing tips for handling important papers:

- *Keep important documents in a safe deposit box.* These include: mortgage documents, real estate deeds, birth and marriage certificates, citizenship papers, and military service records.
- *Create an "active" file.* Place in it unpaid bills, receipt of paid bills, bank statements, and cancelled checks, income tax working papers, records of charitable donations, and so forth.
- *Keep a personal data file* including employment records, credit card information, insurance policies, wills, family health records, social security information.
- *Keep a home maintenance notebook* including appliance manuals and warranties, contractor receipts and warranties.
- *Keep an office notebook* with copies of computer and office equipment manuals, receipts, warranties, or leases.

Avoid using manila file folders stacked in file-cabinet drawers. These flimsy file folders are difficult to find and separate and often slide under one another, making them easy to lose. Use sturdier hanging file folders and file cabinets with high-walled drawers designed to hold these folders. If your file cabinet has regular low-walled drawers, you can buy and easily install adapter brackets to hold the hanging files.

Don't get fancy with file labeling. Use a commonsense labeling scheme and file in alphabetical order. Don't cram files in drawers; this makes them difficult to find and discourages you from even looking. When space gets tight, go through your files and throw away old and obsolete material. Or buy additional file cabinets.

Avoid building stacks of paper on horizontal surfaces. Files should be kept in hanging file folders in a file cabinet or in a series of three-ring binders. If you use binders, label the spines according to the different categories of files (for example, "home," "personal computer," "car," and so forth).

Avoid organizing papers by piling them on your desk. You will quickly clutter your desk and run out of space in which to put fresh stacks. Then you begin putting stacks on top of stacks, which makes it virtually impossible to identify by sight the files in the bottom stacks.

Another flaw of the horizontal-pile filing system is that it can handle an extremely limited amount of files. A typical desk that is 3 feet deep by 7 feet wide, for instance, can only accommodate 30 stacks; if you don't put stacks on stacks; that's a total of only 30 different files.

By comparison, an article in *Law Enforcement Technology* (May, 1998) reports that the average four-drawer file cabinet contains 10,000 pieces of paper. If you have 50 sheets per file, that's a total of 200 files. Therefore, your average four-drawer file cabinet can hold almost seven times more files than the top of a table or desk. And the files in the cabinet can't be knocked over by a breeze or clumsy accident.

With file folders removed from your desk, you'll have room for the few active files you need within reach. To organize these files, set up a double or triple-decker in-basket or a separate small set of files for handling incoming paper. I plan my day so I have time every day to go through incoming papers. This way, I can take care of each piece of paper on the spot. If you let papers pile up in in-baskets or to-do files, you may find yourself missing deadlines, payments, and other commitments. Many of the papers will become too old to be meaningful by the time you get to them. And the growing stacks of papers to attend to will become depressing and disheartening.

Paperwork is a necessary evil. To gain greater control over it, decide what to do with each piece of paper as it comes into your office. Then, get rid of it. Pass it along, file it, sign it, revise it, or throw it out. The key is to take action on it right away. Handle each piece of paper as it comes in, and you'll get things done faster, on time, and with less stress.

For the busy business executive or entrepreneur, better organization of paperwork translates directly into getting more done in less time. Poor organization of paper files wastes time and can result in loss of important materials.

Practice the magic of saying no

Most of us would rather say yes than no. This may be a result of countless "positive thinking" books and seminars from motivational speakers. Or perhaps it's simply inherent in our nature that we want to please. However, to stay organized and to save time each day, you have to learn to say yes less often and no more often. Although it's scary at first, it's liberating both at work and in your personal life once you put this idea into practice.

Why do you need to say no more often? It's simple: the demand on your time generated by all these requests outweighs the supply. If you say yes to everything others ask of you, you'll have no time for yourself or other things that are very important to you.

Worse, the easiest sin in the world to commit is to over-commit oneself. "Saying no can be a very positive thing," writes David MacAdam, pastor of the New Life Church in Concord, Massachusetts. "However, in our culture, it has become a very difficult thing to do." But the penalties for *not* saying no are even tougher: stress, pressure, overwork, and ultimately missed deadlines and the displeasure of the very people you were seeking to please. MacAdam concludes: "By saying no to the trivial, we can say yes to the important" (www.newlife.org/tgim, September 15, 1997).

The New Bedford Police Department provides local teens with advice for saying no to drinking, smoking, and drugs on their Web site: www.ci.newbedford.ma.us/PSAFETY/POLICE. With the minor variations added below, these tactics can be equally effective in the business world as well as in most aspects of your personal life:

- ☾ *Say, "no thanks."* When asked, "Would you like to participate in our committee meeting?" simply reply, "No thanks."

- ☾ *Give a reason.* "Aren't you interested in the committee's work?" your colleague queries. You respond, "Yes, but Tuesday evenings I coach pee-wee soccer" or "I have other commitments."

🕐 *Repeat refusals.* Continue to say no politely but firmly. They'll get the message.

🕐 *Walk away.* "Can you come to this seminar?" a colleague asks as you are both heading in the direction of the corporate training center. "Sorry, but I can't," you say and at the corner where the hallways intersect you start walking the other way.

🕐 *Change the subject.* "Can we go over these numbers now?" your bookkeeper asks when you have other priorities. You reply, "Can you get me the month-to-date sales figures instead?"

🕐 *Give them the cold shoulder.* An effective way to deal with door-to-door and telephone solicitors is simply to say "no thank you" and close the door or hang up the phone.

Ken Blanchard, co-author of the best-selling book *The One-Minute Manager,* has offered these additional tips for saying no that will keep you on track and save you time in the *Executive Edge Newsletter* (1996):

1. Know what your goals and priorities are. If you have a plan for managing your work and time, it is easier to say no to new activities that don't fit into your agenda. I have a saying in one of my programs that goes, "A person who does not have goals is used by someone who does."

Be clear on your priorities. What are you currently trying to accomplish? By when? How can you focus your energy on things that will move you toward those goals? You have to be somewhat inflexible, as a new assignment or opportunity can be a distraction.

Just let your goals become your reality check. To achieve these goals, you need to set priorities and stick with them. Then you will be better able to discern whether opportunities are important for you at this time in your life.

Good performance always starts with clear goals. Without clear goals you will quickly become a victim of having too many commitments. You will have no framework in which to make decisions about where you should or shouldn't focus your energy.

2. Be realistic about the consequences of doing one more thing. This is both for yourself and for the person who wants your time. The best approach is to be honest and direct. For example, say, "If I do this, I won't be able to get to do the other things that I've committed to," or "with what I've got going on right now, I feel certain that I won't do as good a job as I'd like and we will both be disappointed." When a new opportunity comes your way, compliment the idea (if you feel it has merit) before declining to participate.

3. Offer alternatives and solutions. Suggest someone else who you feel could do a better job or who is available sooner to work on the task. If the request is from your manager, suggest a project or priority that you are doing that could be dropped, delayed, or given to someone else, or ask him or her to suggest an alternative plan.

Which approach you use does, of course, depend on who's asking for your commitment, what the task or project is, and the time frame involved. A request from your manager will involve more consideration and discussion than a request from an associate or someone you don't know.

High performers usually focus on only a few things at a time. Peter Drucker asserts that the only people who truly get anything done are monomaniacs—people that intensely focus on one thing at a time. The more you take on, the greater the chance that you will lose effectiveness not only in getting that task done but most likely in all aspects of your life.

Keep in mind that when you say no, you're not saying no to the person, only to the proposition. The people you turn down should not feel insulted. Eleanor Roosevelt said, "Nobody can make you feel inferior without your permission."

There are fates worse than being too busy; one is not being busy enough! For the corporate manager, insufficient workload can spell boredom and be a warning sign that employment is at risk. For the entrepreneur, it can mean slow sales and not enough revenue to meet operating expenses. Being too busy is different from not being busy enough.

Achieve balance

When you learn to organize your life, you'll find that you have more time—more time not only to get things done at work, but also more time for your personal life. But even with this extra time, achieving a balance between work and home life is for many people a constant struggle.

According to a survey by the Heldrich Center for Work Force Development, 87 percent of workers surveyed said the ability to balance work and family was an "extremely important" job factor (*The Record,* September 4, 1998). Since work and family compete for the same limited resource—your time—conflict is inevitable.

> "We must identify those activities that contribute to our well-being," writes Frank Basile in his book *Come Fly With Me* (Charisma Publications). "Then we must exclude all other activities...we will have maximum time to spend doing those things which we have consciously identified as being important."

Statistics suggest some factors compensate naturally for the conflict between family and home life. You might, for example, expect married people, especially those with families, to have less time for work than singles. But according to an article in *Men's Health* magazine (March, 1998), the average married man works 44 hours a week versus 38 hours a week for the average single man. Perhaps the financial burden of supporting a family compels the married worker to put in more hours to ensure success at the office. Or maybe these men stay in the office because it's easier than dealing with problems at home. Whatever the reason, the conflict in balance is apparent.

A key to achieving balance within a limited amount of time is to focus on whatever you are doing at the moment. Don't fret about your weekend date when you're preparing a brief. Don't try to solve work problems in your head while playing a board game with your daughter. "Compartmentalize our different roles," advises Dr. Joyce Brothers in her column in New York's *Daily News* (October 27, 1998). "Then move on to the next task."

When you do tackle problems at work or home, try to find long-term solutions rather than quick fixes and patches. It takes more time up front but can save time in the long run by eliminating repetition of similar problems. "When issues come up, I don't just look to resolve them, I look for solutions so the problems never resurface," says Peter Fioretti, president of Mountain Funding (*Wealth Building*, March, 1998).

Finally, sometimes to achieve balance, you just have to make tough choices: this instead of that. Information systems professional Jim Geisert, in a letter to the editor in *ComputerWorld* (December 14, 1998), writes: "It's been a constant struggle to make managers realize my family is more important to me than the next unrealistic deadline. Has my career suffered for it? Absolutely. But it was worth it. I have a happy, healthy daughter who knows she can count on me to be there when she needs me."

Perhaps the headline on the front cover of the Winter 1999 Day-Timer catalog—which shows a father hugging his toddler son—says it best: "The most productive meeting time isn't always job related."

Some people complain to me, "Being organized is too much work!" And yes, there's effort involved in setting up systems and changing behaviors to become better organized and more time-efficient. But the long-term reward for being organized returns the short-term investment many times over. Richard J. Leider observes in his book *The Power of Purpose* (Berrett-Koehler Publishers, 1997), "Contrary to many people's thinking, to be organized often means the liberation of time and energy, not the cramping of our style."

Chapter 8

Maximizing Your Personal Energy

"Time is as elusive as a thief, silent as death."
—Mumia Abu-Jamal

The pace today is brutal. You need maximum energy just to keep up. Yet most of us don't have enough energy available to fuel the super-productivity we may wish to achieve in the time available to do it.

This energy drain often stems from the growing societal demand to literally make every second count. According to a study from the Future Foundation (a London-based think tank) we are rapidly approaching a 24-hour society. "The World Wide Web, fax machines, and other information technology make it possible to operate around the clock, increasing the pressure to do so," says an article in the *Futurist* (April, 1998). The result is increased customer demand to have services available at all hours.

Coping with this frantic pace can be draining at times. This chapter explores some ideas to help boost your energy level so you can think better and concentrate longer and thus make the most of the time you choose to dedicate to both work and play.

> "The average person puts only 25 percent of his energy and ability to work," Andrew Carnegie complained. "The world takes its hat off to those who put in more than 50 percent of their capacity and stands on its head for those few-and-far-between souls who devote 100 percent" (*Bits & Pieces*, January 28, 1999).

Re-energize yourself

I admit it: I'm tired. Fortunately, I have enough energy to do the one thing I really love to do—work. But I collapse on evenings and weekends. That's not a good thing because I have two active young sons who need my attention. So increasing my energy level is a short-term goal for me.

I know I'm not alone in this situation. Many people I talk to complain that today's fast pace tires them out and robs them of energy. "If energy is the currency of life, many of us have little left in reserve," writes Melissa Diane Smith in her article "Energy to Spare" (*Delicious!*, June, 1997). "We've dipped into our storage bank so often and pushed ourselves so much that we're simply energy depleted."

Here are some ideas for increasing your energy levels:

Get a check-up. As Lauri M. Aesoph observes in her article, "Nutrients that Energize" (*Health & Nutrition Breakthroughs*, April, 1998), "Fatigue is a symptom, not a disease." Therefore, if you suffer from constant fatigue, a trip to your family physician may be a good idea.

Factors that can contribute to low energy include: lack of sleep, stress, poor eating habits, too little water, lack of exercise, and side effects from prescription drugs. Arthritis, heart disease, hypothyroidism, obesity, depression, cancer, and other diseases can also diminish energy.

Do you suffer from chronic fatigue? The causes of Chronic Fatigue Syndrome (CFS) are not well understood. Neither are the treatments. However, as the name implies, those who suffer from CFS are chronically exhausted and need specialized medical attention.

If you are always tired, your physician might also check for mitochondrial dysfunction. Mitochondria supply the body with energy by metabolically breaking down protein, carbohydrate, and fat in cells. A number of factors, including stress, changes in diet, environmental toxins, or over-exertion, can interfere with this energy production.

If you're wasting time every day because you're just too tired to concentrate or focus, see your doctor. There may very well be a medical reason for your fatigue.

Eat light and right. Big meals can make you sleepy. What is the reason? Depending on your diet, 50 to 80 percent of the energy produced by digesting food is consumed by the act of digestion itself. The more energy that digestion takes, the less energy the food provides the rest of your body. It takes more energy to digest cooked and processed food and much less to digest fruits, vegetables, grains, and nuts. Try to eat more of the latter. They're easier on your digestive system and you gain more energy from them. The World Health Organization recommends a daily intake of at least 500 grams of fresh fruit and 500 grams of raw vegetables.

If your diet doesn't give you this amount of fresh food, you can juice the fruits and vegetables. Or you can take concentrated fruits and vegetables in capsule form. (Water is taken out of living fruits and vegetables through a drying process involving vacuum, pressure, and temperature. The remaining dry powder is put in capsules with no chemical additives.)

Diet also effects our adrenal glands, which produce hormones that help balance blood sugar. Blood sugar level determines whether we have the right amount of fuel to meet our varying demands for energy. In situations that demand high energy, such as flight from danger, the adrenals release hormones to generate this additional energy. Fatigue is a major symptom of adrenal dysfunction. Other symptoms include poor sleep, low stamina, inability to concentrate, low immune function, poor digestion, and inability to cope with stress.

You can boost the health of your adrenal glands through diet. Eat a well-balanced diet, with protein, fat, and carbohydrates at each meal. This will promote the healthy production of blood sugar, which helps maintain energy levels.

If you know your diet isn't giving you the nutrients you need to stay sharp, talk to your doctor about taking vitamin and mineral supplements. These can help fill in the gaps and keep you going.

Reduce caffeine and sugar. Caffeine and sugar aren't particularly healthy. However, I admit to using both as short-term energy boosters—in moderation, of course.

Sugar has virtually no nutritional value. Eating sugar tends to rob the body of its nutrient stores. It also causes drastic swings in blood sugar levels, stressing the adrenal glands. Coffee, which can give you a temporary lift in energy, also weakens the adrenals.

Given these facts, here's how I use sugar and caffeine: I know I'm going to consume a certain amount of both anyway. Because they do give a natural energy lift, I eat or drink them at those times I know I want the energy boost they provide, and I avoid them at other times of day.

For instance, like many people, I drink coffee in the morning for the caffeine stimulation. But unlike many people, I don't drink another cup after dinner. After all, why would I want another caffeine shot when I'm relaxing in the evening and getting ready to go to bed?

The approximate caffeine content of popular caffeine-containing foods and drinks are listed below:

Item	Average mg of caffeine
Coffee (5 oz. cup)	
Brewed by drip method	115 mg
Brewed by percolator	80 mg
Instant	65 mg

Item	Average mg of caffeine
Tea (5 oz. cup)	
Brewed	40 mg
Instant	30 mg
Iced (12-oz. cup)	70 mg
Chocolate bar (6 oz.)	25 mg
Chocolate milk (1 oz.)	6 mg
Coca-Cola	46 mg
Excedrin	65 mg
Dristan tablets	16 mg

Reprinted by permission from *Insomnia: 50 Essential Things to Do.* Theresa Foy DiGeronimo (Penguin Group, 1997)

As for sugar, I sometimes have a small candy bar or cookie in the mid-afternoon, the period when my energy most often wanes. But I don't eat candy as a snack at any other time, and I rarely have cookies or cake for dessert. This limited indulgence keeps me happy and at the same time helps me avoid the energy-zapping effects of too much sugar.

Practice feng shui: Energy in the workplace

Can you literally increase your energy by rearranging the furniture in your office? Believe it or not, practitioners of feng shui think so.

Feng shui, a 3,000-year-old, Chinese discipline for harmonious interior design, has had a stateside revival in recent years and is transforming the surroundings of business executives across the country. What some may regard as New Age touchy-feely nonsense has been embraced wholeheartedly by the likes of Donald Trump, Tommy Hilfiger, Madonna, and Steve Martin. In the workplace, the teachings of feng shui (pronounced FUNG SHWAY) are improving employee relations and increasing overall productivity.

"When people call me, they want to increase their profits and their prosperity," says Carole Bollini, a consultant who runs

Enlightened Environment in Oakland, New Jersey. By adding foliage or water fountains, by repositioning furniture or by reconstructing entire rooms, feng shui consultants and their clients try to lift and guide spirits to produce results (*Business News,* January 18, 1999).

The term *feng shui* translates into English as wind and water. The teachings center around the notion that the design of a room can represent a particular theme, such as relationships, careers, or prosperity. It is used to affect personal emotions and energy, which, according to feng shui philosophy, flow like the wind and water, in a positive way.

The art began to appear in the U.S. about 10 years ago in California, where it was introduced by migrating Chinese masters. "It's just beginning to come into more focus on the East Coast," says Bollini, who has been a practicing consultant since 1996. Here are some of the principles of this art:

🕐 *Water.* "Water fountains are placed in the front entrance of a business or to the left to enhance the career section of the room," says Valerie Bogdan, a consultant who runs Feng Shui Works out of her Somerset home. Each year, Bogdan advises 15 corporate clients, including AT&T and Merrill Lynch, 100 small business owners, and 200 homeowners. "Water is a sign of prosperity and generates a relaxed calm connection to nature," she adds (*Business News,* January 18, 1999).

🕐 *Space.* One practice of feng shui is known as space clearing—basically the philosophy of out with the old and in with the new. Articles of furniture and miscellaneous items that are cluttering space are removed and the consultant clears the area of negative energies by walking around the room to spread the fumes from smoldering sage sticks. The pleasing scent and the removal of old junk infuses positive energy into the room. "Clutter," says Bollini, "causes stagnation."

Space constraints can also have a negative impact on employee motivation, according to Bollini. "Being surrounded by computers, squashing too many people into too small a room, and not having a connection to nature is negative," she says. "Also, sitting with your back to the door makes you subconsciously think about being surprised and that is a drain on energy."

🕒 *Art.* Bogdan sometimes needs to help her clients liven up their walls. "Some of the artwork at corporations is cold and hostile. They will have abstract or very confusing pictures. I find that to be the most negative," says Bogdan. To ease employee spirits she recommends images of lighthearted and nature-oriented scenes, such as children playing or sunsets.

🕒 *Light.* Lighting also plays a factor on the state of mind, according to both Bollini and Bogdan. They find that the oppressive feel of fluorescent lighting can be countered with full spectrum light. That gives the effect of true daylight indoors, thus bringing a sense of nature back into the workplace.

Monitor your sleep

Numerous studies indicate that most people need eight hours of sleep; yet an increasing number get far less. We are working longer, staying up later, and getting up earlier. For instance, the Future Foundation study found a 20-percent increase in British television viewing between 3 a.m. and 6 a.m.(*The Futurist,* April, 1998). The result is an increasing number of people who can't focus. Anyone who has ever pulled an "all nighter" to cram for an exam or a presentation knows that sleep deprivation dulls your mental edge.

Workers who sleep less so they can work more and get more done may in fact be accomplishing the opposite. The National Sleep Foundation estimates overtired employees cost American business $18 billion annually in errors and slowness (*Forbes,* December 14, 1998).

A major cause of poor sleep among busy professionals is *ruminating,* which is the practice of thinking about work problems when you're not at work. Many professionals I have talked with tell me that Sunday night is miserable for them because all they do is think about the problems they have to deal with on Monday morning. They toss and turn and get little sleep. Some even say work nightmares dominate their dreams!

What's the solution? Clear your mind of all your worries before you go to bed each night. Writing in *Professional Speaker* (March, 1998), Angela Brown suggests you make a list of things on your mind, leave that list on your nightstand, and don't allow yourself to think about any of them until morning. "Once you release your have-tos and should-haves from your conscious mind, you'll enjoy a deeper sleep," says Brown. "When you awaken, you'll be refreshed and ready to tackle the list with renewed enthusiasm."

My sister Fern has a different solution for coping with her Sunday-night worries: She often goes into the office for a few hours Sunday night. "I'm going to worry anyway, so while this stuff is on my mind, I'd rather be at my desk getting it organized and done," says Fern. An added benefit of Fern's Sunday night work session is a reduced workload for Monday mornings, which in turn helps lower her stress levels.

Here are some additional tips for getting a good night's sleep:

- ☺ Drink no more than five cups of caffeinated drinks a day and none in the four hours before bedtime.

- ☺ Cut down on smoking. Nicotine is a central nervous system stimulant that can make it difficult to fall asleep and because it's addictive, cravings may wake you in the middle of the night.

- ☺ Avoid a nightcap. Alcohol has an initial sedative effect. However it causes arousals and sleep fragmentation during the night that lower the quality and restorative power of sleep.

- ☺ Beware of the sleep-disturbing effects of many over-the-counter and prescription drugs. Medications that can disrupt sleep include those that contain caffeine, such as Excedrin, Anacin, or Triaminic, many antidepressant drugs, some birth-control pills, some bronchodilating drugs for asthma, steroid preparations, some drugs for high blood pressure, and many diet pills.

🕐 Try to keep a consistent daily schedule. Rise and sleep at the same time every day.

🕐 Stay away from sleeping pills. These pills cause tolerance, which requires you to use more and more for the same effect. They can increase sleeplessness when they are discontinued. And they can be addictive and cause withdrawal symptoms when they are discontinued.

Try relaxation techniques

Relaxation techniques are activities that help you relax when you want to so that you can recharge your batteries and have energy when you need to.

There are many ways to relax. Stephen King, the best-selling horror novelist, reads fiction to unwind. "People sometimes overlook the restorative power of stories," said King in a speech at a bookseller's convention I attended.

Fiction is escape—and relaxation. Most popular forms of entertainment—books, videos, movies, TV shows—are based around stories. Even most rock songs tell a story and most video games have a plot. So the right relaxation technique for you might be as simple as curling up with a good mystery.

Some people practice yoga—known for its ability to reduce stress and increase mental discipline and concentration—to relax. "The word 'yoga' conjures up many images, including emaciated Indians in contorted postures, swallowing rags, levitating above the ground, and meditating for unreasonably long periods of time," says yoga teacher Kathleen Miller. "In reality, yoga is a physical discipline involving particular postures and possibly some breathing techniques."

In the United States the most common yoga practice is hatha yoga, which involves mainly the body and breath. According to Miller, hatha yoga's effects of relaxation, increased flexibility, strength, vitality, improved concentration and immune system function have been well-documented.

Another very popular relaxation technique is Transcendental Meditation (TM). According to books and literature from the

Maharishi Vedic University, the TM technique is a simple, natural, effortless procedure practiced for 15-20 minutes in the morning and evening, while sitting comfortably with the eyes closed (www.maharishi.org).

During TM, the individual experiences a unique state of restful alertness. As the body becomes relaxed, the mind transcends all mental activity to experience the simplest form of awareness, called "Transcendental Consciousness." Practitioners claim that this practice dissolves accumulated stress and fatigue through the deep rest gained during the practice. This, in turn, helps practitioners achieve greater effectiveness and success in daily life.

The Vedic University reports that more than 500 scientific research studies conducted during the past 25 years at more than 200 independent universities and research institutes in 30 countries have shown that the TM program benefits all areas of an individual's life: mind, body, behavior, and environment. The research has been published in numerous scientific journals including *Science, Scientific American,* and the *International Journal of Neuroscience.*

10 ways to reduce stress

Life can be a pressure cooker. Too much stress not only harms personal productivity; it can be costly too. A survey by the Health Enhancement Research Organization reveals that people who said they were under constant stress had medical expenditures 46 percent higher than people without such stress, which cost businesses an extra $2,287 a year each per employee (*American Demographics,* February, 1999).

In addition to the relaxation techniques mentioned earlier, here are 10 simple techniques you can use to reduce stress and tension.

1. *Hobbies.* The best way to take your mind off your work is with a hobby that fills your free time. Pick a hobby that offers you something you can't get on the job. For example, if you sit at a desk all day, try hiking, camping, bicycle riding or some other physical activity. If you feel your job

doesn't provide an outlet for your creativity, take up painting, music or another activity that satisfies your creative side.

2. *Vacations.* Many people boast of going years without a vacation. But this is a sign of trouble—not commitment. Sitting on the beach, under the sun, with the waves pounding at your feet is a marvelous way to let off some of the pressure that builds up in the work environment.

   A study from Hyatt Hotels & Resorts (*Sales & Marketing Management*, March 1999), revealed that 63 percent of executives said periodic, one-week vacations were essential to maintaining a positive attitude at work. In fact, 73 percent of executives surveyed said they'd rather pass up a 10-percent pay raise than give up a week of vacation time.

   How long should your vacation be? It depends on your personality. Some people find they need at least a week or two to unwind fully. Others say taking that much time off creates a backlog of work that just adds to their stress when they return to the job. Those people may be better off with several short vacations throughout the year.

3. *Screening.* If you find constant interruptions stressful, it may pay to screen calls and visitors. Take calls when you want to; if you're busy, have someone take a message so you can return the call later.

4. *Unlisted phone number.* Few things are as intrusive as a work-related phone call received at home. If you are bothered by too many such calls from subordinates or supervisors, consider getting an unlisted number. If company policy dictates that people at work must have access to your home number, you might want to buy a telephone answering machine or let voice mail pick up your incoming calls (then retrieve the message and decide whether to respond). Another option is to get Caller ID. When the phone rings, the LED shows who the call is from. Then you decide whether to take it or let the voice mail answer.

5. *Privacy.* Modular offices and open work spaces are popular with managers who think constant employee interaction is a good thing. But these setups deprive workers of privacy

and lack of privacy in turn adds stress and reduces productivity. You should consider an office setup in which all your employees have small, private offices, with doors they can easily shut. Small inner offices give each employee a quiet place to think.

6. *Dual offices.* My Uncle Max, a college professor, has two offices: his regular office and a small, "secret" office tucked away in the basement of another department's building. Max goes to the hidden office to unwind and to work away from the crowds for a few hours when the pressures of students, faculty meetings, and research begin to overwhelm him.

7. *Delegation.* Do you have too much work to do? Delegate it. Don't think you're the only one who can do your work. You'd be surprised at what your co-workers can accomplish for you.

8. *Divide and conquer.* If you're faced with a big task and a short deadline, break the assignment up into many smaller segments and do a part of the job every day. Having to write only one page a day for 10 days seems a lot less formidable a task than having to produce a 10-page paper in two weeks.

9. *Deep breathing.* Psychologists have developed a number of relaxation techniques that can help reduce stress on the job. All these techniques can be performed easily at work. One of the most basic techniques is deep breathing. It relieves stress and tension by increasing your oxygen intake. To practice it, sit in a comfortable position with your hands on your stomach. Inhale deeply and slowly. Let your stomach expand as much as possible. Hold your breath for five seconds. Then, exhale slowly through pursed lips, as if you were whistling. Repeat the cycle three or four times.

10. *Visualizations.* To escape from the stress of the "real world" close your door, sit back and spend the next 10 minutes in a pleasant daydream. This short "mental vacation" provides a nice tension-reducing break.

Use productive energy in intense, short bursts

In Chapter 1, we talked about the strategy of breaking your day into one-hour work segments. In addition to organizing your activity for the day, the "hour power" method has another benefit: it gives you added energy to get more done.

One or two hours turns out to be the perfect work increment: It seems to be the optimum period of time for working with intense concentration. Why? Research shows that you suffer a loss of stamina after 90 to 120 minutes of focused activity. After that time, the body needs a break to induce the biological changes that restore energy.

With this method, not only do you maximize your energy, you focus it on one task. The result is you make significant headway on that task in only one to two hours. The breaks between your intense work sessions need not be long; two to five minutes can re-energize you for the next one or two hours.

With this method of maximizing energy, you make every second count for a specific block of time, then recharge and get back to productive work. This is a great time-management technique that uses both intense and relaxed time to complement each other.

After the last hour of intense work, mentally reward yourself with a break—for the entire evening. Don't carry around the burdens of work after you have left your office for the night. Write them on tomorrow's to-do list, post them, and be done with it. When you're at rest, really rest.

"Finish every day and be done with it," advised the poet Ralph Waldo Emerson. "You have done what you could. Some blunders and absurdities no doubt crept in; but get rid of them and forget them as soon as you can. Tomorrow is a new day, and you should never encumber its potentialities and invitation with the dread of the past. You should not waste a moment of today on the rottenness of yesterday."

Don't Worry

The strategies offered in this chapter should help you re-energize yourself, relax, and reduce stress. All of these things will drastically reduce the amount of time you spend worrying. Worrying saps your energy and rarely solves problems. Productive people spend their energy doing something about their problems rather than just worrying about them.

"Keep worrying in your life to a minimum," advises Reverend Louis Conselatore in an article in *Inner Realm.* His top three reasons to leave your worries behind are:

1. *Worrying is futile and impotent.* Studies have found that 40 percent of our worries relate to things that never occur, 30 percent to things we cannot change, 12 percent to health (while we are still healthy), and 10 percent to petty concerns. Only 8 percent of worries are about real problems. Thus, 92 percent of our worries are wasted.

2. *Worrying is like looking at life through a dense fog.* The total moisture in a dense fog 100 feet high covering seven city blocks can fit into a glass of water. If we see our problems in their true light, they can be relegated to their true size and place. "And if all our worries were reduced to their true size, you could probably stick them into a water glass too," Conselatore writes.

3. *Worrying is bad for your health.* A recent Mayo Clinic study revealed that 80 percent to 85 percent of their patients were ill directly or indirectly because of mental stress.

There can be a thrill in being super-productive—especially in a culture where busyness and accomplishment are status symbols. But watch out. You're not superman or superwoman. You need time to rest and recharge. Don't sacrifice long-term performance for short-term gain. Take care of yourself.

Chapter 9

Managing Information Overload

"We are now so preoccupied with keeping up with the bombardment of new facts, new developments, and new points of view that we have no time to listen to the past, or reflect on even the most recent history, much less to make a judicious reckoning of its significance."
—Regis McKenna, public relations specialist

As Richard Saul Wurman points out in his book *Information Anxiety* (Doubleday, 1989), more information has been produced in the last 30 years than in the previous 5,000. Everyone has too much to read and is drowning in data. A radio commercial for the *Dilbert* cartoon show has Dilbert's voice mail saying, "You have 947 messages...all of them urgent." This is an exaggeration, but not by much. According to an article in *Men's Health* magazine (September, 1997), the typical Fortune 1,000 employee sends and receives 178 messages each day!

An article called "Information is bad for you, says Reuters report" (Reuters press release, October 14, 1996) shows that an excess of information is "strangling businesses and causing personnel to suffer mental anguish and physical illness, as well as having a detrimental effect on relationships and leisure time." More than half of the 1,313 managers questioned in the survey agreed they needed high levels of information to perform effectively; one in four also admitted to suffering ill health as a result of the amount of information they now handle. Worse, 94 percent of managers do not believe that the situation will improve and 56 percent feel that the future will be even more stressful.

Other key findings of the survey:

- Two-thirds of managers report that tension with work colleagues and loss of job satisfaction arise because of stress associated with information overload.

- One third of managers suffer from ill health as a direct consequence of stress associated with information overload. This figure rises to 43 percent among senior managers.

- Almost two thirds (62 percent) of managers testify that their personal relationships suffer as a result of information overload.

- More than four out of 10 managers think that important decisions are delayed and the ability to make decisions affected as a result of having far too much information.

- One in five senior managers believe that substantial amounts of time are wasted collecting and searching for information.

- Almost half think that the Internet will be a prime cause of information overload over the next two years.

This chapter presents strategies for coping with this information overload. The key is to "filter" and be selective in your information intake, rather than comprehensive. It's impossible to gather and analyze all the information related to your work, and doing so would leave you no time to accomplish your necessary tasks.

Reduce information input

Many of my clients are newsletter and magazine publishers and I spend a good part of my time convincing their subscribers to renew. But from a practical, time-management point of view, perhaps you should be getting fewer periodicals than you do.

The problem with periodicals is that they come when delivered, not necessarily when you need them or have time to read them. A book can be put aside on the shelf for future reference, but a periodical demands more immediate attention. Getting a lot of periodicals in the mail can be stressful; you feel compelled to read or at least skim them all. Therefore, you can cut your information overload stress—and reading burden—by getting fewer rather than more publications.

Here's a good way to determine whether you really need a publication: When the renewal notices come, ignore them and let the subscription run out. Then evaluate your life for a few weeks without the periodical. If you don't miss it, you just eliminated information overload from your life. If you do miss it, simply reactivate your subscription.

> Many publishers give former subscribers (called "expires") a special lower rate if they resubscribe within a certain period of time.

Don't read—scan

I get quite a bit of mail each day. People in my office building see this and ask me, "How do you have time to read all the magazines and newsletters you get?" The secret is: I don't read it. Instead, I scan. Here's how you too can save time by scanning instead of reading, without missing important information:

🕐 For many of us, the daily news has minimal affect on our day-to-day work. Therefore, it's unnecessary to read the majority of the articles and bulletins that cross your desk. I skip more than 90 percent of them every day.

⊕ I scan periodicals for article titles that are relevant to my current interests and projects. Skipping the non-relevant articles, I turn to the relevant articles and scan them rapidly.

⊕ If the article contains relevant and useful information, such as a good quote, an interesting statistic, a useful method, or an idea, I clip it. When cutting the article out, be sure to write the name of the periodical, date of publication, and page number on all of your clippings. This way, you know the source of the information if you want to use it later on. Also, use a pen or yellow highlighter to highlight the one or two pieces of key information that motivated you to clip and save the article in the first place.

⊕ After I clip articles, some are dropped into reference or project files for immediate or future use. If, say, I am working on a book on the Internet, I drop articles about the Internet I have clipped into that file. I also keep general files for topics I write or consult on frequently, such as computers, pollution control, finance, health care, and so forth.

⊕ Others clippings that I find may be more of interest to colleagues than to me. I pass them on as a service. If I want to send an article to my colleague Ron Fry, publisher of Career Press, I write at the top of the article in pen, "RF—FYI—Bob Bly." I then put a note on the article with the instructions, "Mail to Ron Fry" and give it to my secretary, Carolyn. Doing so lets me correspond with clients and colleagues in a meaningful way. And the best part is that it takes only a few seconds to make each correspondence.

⊕ To avoid clutter, I don't save periodicals after I have read them. Instead, I throw them out (actually, I recycle them). If I need an article, I'll clip and file it for reference. You can also scan articles and store them on your computer.

Cut the "info fat" from your data diet

Most of the information that you and I take in daily is a huge waste of our time. We do it either out of habit or because we enjoy it. If you enjoy it, continue to absorb it, but recognize it's a luxury and not a necessity. If you do it out of habit—for instance, your parents read a daily newspaper and watched the evening news every night, so you do to—consider breaking that habit. Doing so can save you a considerable amount of time each day.

Most of the information we're trained to absorb is largely irrelevant, both to our business and personal lives. So much news is either sensational or celebrity-focused—in a word, interesting on a gossip level but unimportant on a practical level. As journalist David Halberstam observes:

> We've morphed ourselves steadily from a Calvinist society to an entertainment society. We've become a less serious one—and a more coarse one. You can see this in the explosion of tabloid TV shows and in the changed agenda every night on the news. It's the power of images over words.
>
> When I was a young man, a great [newspaper] editor was someone who balanced what people wanted to know with what they needed to know. There's less and less of that all the time. The great sin these days is not to be wrong; it's to be boring. It's about ratings.
>
> There is a stunning rise in popular culture. We've seen the "Hollywoodization" of our society, the rise of the celebrity culture, and the canonization of people who are not very interesting, are not very important, and have almost nothing to say, into major figures.

Gossip, celebrity, and news once were our fascination because following them provided an entertaining activity to combat boredom in our daily lives. Now that we are so busy, we don't have those empty hours to fill; yet we continue to obsess over the latest White House scandal or Hollywood marriage crisis. Why? Force of habit. Gossip, celebrity, and news used to be the means to an end (eliminating boredom);

now they have become the ends in themselves. That's a bad thing for people who have better things to do.

The bottom line: Save time by cutting low-content media from your diet. Or at least make sure the content is useful to you in some way. My personal philosophy when evaluating information resources is: If you don't think you'll use it, lose it.

Improve your listening skills

The success of many of our business activities depends on how well we listen. Studies show that we spend about 80 percent of our waking hours communicating, and at least 45 percent of that time listening. If you are listening at only 50-percent efficiency, you are wasting 22.5 percent of your time.

Although listening is so critical in our daily lives, it is taught and studied far less than the other three basic communications skills: reading, writing, and speaking. Much of the trouble we have communicating with others is because of poor listening skills. "What I've noticed is that people not being good listeners, looking at their watch in a conversation or during a meeting," says etiquette consultant Sue Fox (*ComputerWorld,* March 1, 1999). "If people don't have the time or interest in meeting with someone, they just shouldn't do it."

The good news is that listening efficiency can be improved by understanding the steps involved in the listening process and by following these basic guidelines.

Are you a good listener? Most people are not. Sperry, a company that has built its corporate identity around the theme of good listening, reports that 85 percent of all people questioned rated themselves average or less in listening ability. Fewer than 5 percent rated themselves either superior or excellent.

You can imagine where you fall in this spectrum by thinking about your relationships with the people in your life: your boss, colleagues, subordinates, best friend, spouse. If asked, what would they say about how well you listen? Do you often misunderstand assignments or only vaguely remember what people have said to you? If so, you may need to improve your listening skills.

The listening process involves four basic steps:

1. *Hearing is the first step in the process.* At this stage, you simply pay attention to make sure you have heard the message. If your boss says, "McGillicudy, I need the report on last month's sales" and you can repeat the sentence, then you have heard her.

2. *The second step is interpretation.* Failure to interpret the speaker's words correctly frequently leads to misunderstanding. People sometimes interpret words differently because of varying experience, knowledge, vocabulary, culture, background, and attitudes.

   A good speaker uses tone of voice, facial expressions, and mannerisms to help make the message clear to the listener. For instance, if your boss speaks loudly, frowns, and puts her hands on her hips, you know she is probably upset and angry.

3. *Step three: evaluate.* Decide what to do with the information you have received. For example, when listening to a sales pitch, you have two options: You choose either to believe or to disbelieve the salesperson. The judgments you make in the evaluation stage are a crucial part of the listening process.

4. *The final step is to respond to what you have heard.* This is a verbal or visual response that lets the speaker know whether you have gotten the message and what your reaction is. When you tell the salesperson that you want to place an order, you are showing that you have heard and believe his message.

When it comes to listening, many of us are guilty of at least a few bad habits. For example:

- Instead of listening, do you think about what you're going to say next while the other person is still talking?

- Are you easily distracted by the speaker's mannerisms or by what is going on around you?

🕐 Do you frequently interrupt people before they have finished talking?

🕐 Do you drift off into daydreams because you think you know what the speaker is going to say?

All of these habits can hinder our listening ability. Contrary to popular notion, listening is not a passive activity. It requires full concentration and active involvement, and it is in fact rather hard work.

The following tips can help you become a better listener:

🕐 *Don't talk; listen.* Studies show that job applicants are more likely to make a favorable impression and get a job offer when they let the interviewer do most of the talking. This demonstrates that people appreciate a good listener more than they do a good talker.

Why is this so? Because people want a chance to get their own ideas and opinions across. A good listener lets them do it. If you interrupt the speaker or put limitations on your listening time, the speaker will get the impression that you're not interested in what he is saying—even if you are. So be courteous and give the speaker your full attention.

This technique can help you win friends, supporters, and sales. Says master salesman Frank Bettger, "I no longer worry about being a brilliant conversationalist. I simply try to be a good listener. I notice that people who do that are usually welcome wherever they go" (*How I Raised Myself From Failure to Success in Selling*, Prentice Hall, 1970).

🕐 *Don't jump to conclusions.* Many people tune out a speaker when they think they have the gist of his conversation or know what he's trying to say next. Assumptions can be dangerous. Maybe the speaker is not following the same train of thought that you are or is not planning to make the point you think he is. If you don't listen, you may miss the real point the speaker is trying to get across.

🕐 *Listen "between the lines."* Concentrate on what is not being said as well as what is being said. Remember, a lot of clues to meaning come from the speaker's tone of voice, facial expressions, and gestures. People don't always say what they mean, but their body language is usually an accurate indication of their attitude and emotional state.

🕐 *Ask questions.* If you are not sure what the speaker is saying, ask. It's perfectly acceptable to say, "Do you mean...?" or "Did I understand you to say...?" It's also a good idea to repeat what the speaker has said in your own words to confirm that you have understood her correctly.

🕐 *Don't let yourself be distracted by the environment or by the speaker's appearance, accent, mannerisms, or word use.* It's sometimes difficult to overlook a strong accent, a twitch, sexist language, a fly buzzing around the speaker's head, and similar distractions. But paying too much attention to these distractions can break your concentration and make you miss important parts of the conversation.

If outside commotion is a problem, try to position yourself away from it. Make eye contact with the speaker, and force yourself to focus on the message and not on the environment.

🕐 *Keep an open mind.* Don't just listen for statements that back up your own opinions and support your beliefs, or only for certain parts that interest you. The point of listening, after all, is to gain new information.

🕐 *Be willing to listen to someone else's point of view and ideas.* A subject that may seem boring or trivial at first can turn out to be fascinating if you listen with an open mind.

🕐 *Take advantage of your brain power.* You can think approximately four times faster than the listener can talk. So, when you are listening, use this extra brainpower to evaluate what has been said and summarize the central ideas in your own mind. That way, you'll be better prepared to answer any questions or criticisms the speaker poses and you'll be able to communicate with the speaker much more effectively.

🕐 *Provide feedback.* Make eye contact with the speaker. Show him you understand his talk by nodding your head, maintaining an upright posture, and, if appropriate, interjecting an occasional comment such as "I see" or "that's interesting" or "really." The speaker will appreciate your interest and feel that you are really listening.

Motivation is an essential key to becoming a good listener. Think how your ears perk up if someone says, "Let me tell you how pleased I am with that report you did," or "I'm going to reorganize your department and you are in line for a promotion."

Once you've mastered the skill of active listening, you might wish everyone you speak to used the same tools. What can you do when you're the speaker and you want your listener's full attention? Here are a few tips.

🕐 *Make eye contact.* If you're speaking to a group, try directing your attention to various people in the room, one at a time. Make eye contact and speak directly to the person for a minute or so.

🕐 *Avoid a monotone.* Speak clearly. Vary your voice to keep people interested. An inaudible or droning voice can quickly put your listener to sleep figuratively and literally. By varying the inflections in your voice and speaking enthusiastically, you can command greater listener attention.

🕐 *Ask questions.* Whether they are rhetorical or demand some kind of response, questions keep listeners involved. When it comes to communicating, a two-way conversation is usually much more effective than a lecture.

🕐 *Be brief.* Don't be gabby. Get to the point. Avoid wandering off on tangents, stick to the subject at hand. If you are continuing a discussion from a previous meeting, summarize the main points and any conclusions that were reached, so that the current session can be more productive.

🕐 *Choose a location with minimal distractions and interruptions.* If your phone is always ringing, hold important meetings in a conference room away from the office. Doing so keeps people focused on the conversation instead of other activities.

🕐 *Summarize and emphasize key ideas with examples and audiovisual aids.* Examples help clarify your message and show listeners practical applications of your ideas. Slides, overhead projectors, blackboards, or photocopied handouts grab the listener's interest by helping him or her visualize your ideas.

> Strong listening skills are vital tools to add to your collection of time-management skills. Use them daily!

More tips for handling information overload

1. *Be selective.* The Reuters report cited at the beginning of this chapter correctly observes, "People create and distribute because they can, not because they think it's useful." Desktop publishing, for example, has enabled individuals to more easily, write, typeset, and publish their own books; this has resulted in a flood of more books, but not necessarily better books. Look at the amount of useless e-mail—mostly widely distributed bad jokes—you get each day for further proof. Do not create or disseminate information or communications simply because it's easy. Only create information that achieves an objective—yours, the recipient's, or both.

2. *Subscribe to a customized news/data service.* There are a small but growing number of services that deliver "customized news"—usually via fax or e-mail—to their subscribers on a daily basis. One such "free" service is MSNBC (Microsoft NBC). Viewers who want more details on stories can get them on the MSNBC Web site: www.msnbc.com. CNN recently partnered with database giant Oracle to create CNN's Custom News Service. Also available free on the Web (customnews.cnn.com), the CNN Custom News Service lets subscribers set up a profile of the type of news they would like to read. Then, through a custom online clipping service, it sends articles and releases on the topics indicated. There is also a powerful search engine to let you find additional articles on topics not covered in your profile or clipping service.

3. *Get your voice mail under control.* Recently I was in a client's office as he listened to his voice mail messages on speaker phone. As soon as a message began, if it was not a person he knew or not a subject he was interested in, he punched the delete button as fast as a mongoose striking a cobra. One way to save time in listening to voice mail is to politely but firmly request that callers leave a detailed message, not just their name and numbers. You can add that calls without messages may not be returned. Telephone tag is a particularly irksome waste of time and it is inefficient. When you can't reach someone, don't extend the phone tag by leaving just a name, phone number, and call-me message. Say what you want and specify the response you are seeking. This enables the other party to respond fully even if they can't reach you personally and again get your voice mail instead.

4. *Reduce your e-mail correspondence.* With time, e-mail users learn when a response is required and when it is just a waste of electricity and bytes. Avoid sending trivial e-mails such as "thanks" and "you're welcome" and "my pleasure." Cut down on casual e-mails, because it will generate more e-mail—much of it requesting a response—in return. Lynn Lively, author of *Managing*

Information Overload (Amacom), has another suggestion: Don't print your e-mail address on your business cards. "I give my e-mail address only to those I want to hear from every day," says Lively. Delete spam and other messages that are obviously promotional and nonpersonal. Ask to be removed from any e-mail transmissions or subscriptions you don't want, such as Internet newsletters or company bulletins from vendors and potential suppliers. When you send e-mail, write short messages; you will get short messages in return. When you want to end e-mail exchanges with another person, simply don't reply.

5. *Protect yourself.* Refuse to accept information input you deem unimportant or irrelevant. Example: A salesperson from a store where we were buying new kitchen cabinets called to discuss some facet of our order or installation. I said, "Just a minute; let me put my wife on the phone," since the kitchen cabinets are her project and she is the one who knows the details and is interested in its progress. But no, the salesman insisted on giving me the details—none of which I cared one whit about. Finally, Amy walked into the room. I cut him off politely but firmly, said "Here's my wife; talk to her," gave Amy the phone, and left the room. "You don't care about this!" Amy complained to me later. She's right: I don't. I have limited time and too many tasks. I have to set priorities—we all do—and kitchen cabinets simply are not (and never will be) on my priority list.

To overcome this threat to your personal productivity, be highly selective in what you scan, browse, acquire, and otherwise take in. Limit your research and reading to a handful of clearly defined topics in which you know the investment in information acquisition will pay off for you. Jettison the rest. Or if you don't, at least limit reading outside these core categories to things you truly enjoy.

6. *Specify your desired content level.* Frequently people communicating with you give you much more information than you need to make a decision. This is a major time waster and a constant source of annoyance for me. The reason people give too much information is they don't know how much you need. To cut down on information overload, tell them what you require.

7. *Cleanse and purge frequently.* Books, for example, become irrelevant either because they're out of date or the subject matter is no longer of interest to you. I go through my office book shelves frequently, and my rule of thumb is this: Any book I haven't looked at for a year or more I automatically get rid of (usually I send it to a colleague whom I think would enjoy it). As information ages, its value declines (unlike real estate, which is often the opposite). Go through information resources periodically—paper files, electronic files, books, reference manuals—and get rid of whatever is old or irrelevant. The reduced clutter will remove some of the stress caused by information overload. And, you'll have easier access to the remaining information because there's less to search through.

8. *Combine information input with another activity.* Standing in line at the bank is a waste of time, yet it is sometimes a necessity with no alternative choice. But if you read a newsletter or business report while standing in line, you convert that wasted time to productive time. You can watch the news on TV while your family is shopping for a new CD player in the electronics section of the department store. You can listen to a lecture or a book-on-tape while you mow the lawn or do the grocery shopping. You can read a newsletter while sitting idle in a line to get your car inspected.

9. *Know when you have enough information.* When you're making decisions, don't agonize over the fact that you don't have all the information. You never will. Productive people develop an instinct for when it's time to stop

researching and reading, and to start doing and acting. If you don't, you'll spend all your time in the library and not get anything done.

If you're still not convinced that managing information overload is critical to time management, try this experiment: Buy the Sunday *New York Times*. Start reading every word of every article and advertisement. Call me when you finish (I've got lots of time to wait) and we'll talk about how much time you've lost and what it cost you in productivity to take in that much information (most of it useless to your needs). When you learn to skim, scan, and choose selectively, you'll find you have much more time in every day to do the things you always thought you never had time for.

Chapter 10

Off-loading and Priority Management

"The march of time has been replaced by the blitz of time, and no one, short of a hermit, can escape the pace without some sort of defensive personal philosophy."
—Ralph Nader, consumer advocate

Perhaps the most powerful strategy for having more time and getting important things done is to avoid doing things that waste your time. "Off-loading" means purging noncritical tasks from your daily schedule so you can work with focus on things that are high on your priority list. This chapter discusses some tips and techniques for doing just that.

You have heard the expression "a tremendous burden was lifted off his (or her) shoulders." That's what it feels like when you learn to off-load. The key points to keep in mind:

- 🕐 You don't have to do everything everybody tells you to do.
- 🕐 You don't have to do everything the way other people tell you to do it.

🕐 You don't have to do everything always according to the other person's time frame. (My colleague Dan Kennedy is fond of telling clients who want to force rush jobs on him because of their own poor planning: "Your crisis does not automatically become my crisis.")

🕐 You don't always have to do everything yourself. Many other people can do them as well as you can...or if not, at least well enough.

🕐 Being busy does not make you successful. Getting things done does.

🕐 Yes, you have to please other people. But you also have to please yourself.

Master these simple principles of off-loading and you will progress further toward your goal of effective time management.

Pick and choose wisely

A colleague recently complained to me that he didn't have enough time to do everything he had to do. My advice to him? Then don't do it all. You can't. Pick what's essential. Do what's a priority to you and off-load the rest.

The number of things that "must" be done is infinite, but your time is not. You have to reduce your activities down to a finite, manageable number; otherwise, not even the most sophisticated time management techniques can save you.

When you trim your priority list to the essentials, you have a smaller more manageable list, and you know everything on the list is essential. These factors motivate you to diligently work on the items on the list.

"Keeping things simple means not working on a hundred deals at once," writes Robert Ringer in *Looking Out For #1* (Fawcett Crest). "Being a writer has taught me the importance of not getting sidetracked, regardless of how good something else looks. I concur completely with General Patton in that you must be single-minded and drive for the one thing on which you've decided. You can't have all the candy in the candy store, so the sooner you face that reality, the quicker you can get down to the business of making money instead of chaos."

To determine whether to accept or decline an invitation, assignment, or task, ask yourself the following questions:

- Is this task something I want to do?

- Will doing the task help me achieve my business or personal goals?

- Is it something I have to do? Or is it something someone else can do?

- Do I have the time to do it?

- Am I willing to pay the price (in giving up my precious time) to accomplish the task?

- Will doing it make me bored, unhappy, or even miserable?

- Is this the kind of work I do best? Or is the task better suited for another person?

- Can I add value to the task? Or is it something anybody could do?

- Will the benefits of doing the task (the fee, commission, goodwill, customer satisfaction) outweigh the cost (in time and effort)?

- If I had only a year to live and could select only a short list of activities to do, would this be on it?

- Am I willing to accept the consequences (lack of promotion, loss of a customer, decreased sales) that not doing the task may incur?

When you answer these questions, you'll have a task list that includes only those things that are important to you. In her book *Unclutter Your Personal Life* (Carol Publishing), Susan Wright gives these tips for setting and sticking to priorities:

🕐 Do first what will benefit you the most. Why waste time with little or no return? Assess each situation and task according to its reward factor, as well as the damage it could do if left undone.

🕐 Once you have made the decision to take action, don't allow yourself to be pushed into anything. If you have something more important to do, then do it without getting sidetracked.

🕐 Take care of the things that won't last much longer. If you have a limited window of opportunity and it's something you need, give it priority over less immediate tasks.

🕐 Learn to tell the difference between what you "should" do and what you need to do. Often what you "should" do is not what best serves you.

🕐 Take care of the people who can help you or hurt you, whether it's your spouse or your boss, a customer or a co-worker. The people who can most seriously affect your project should be dealt with first.

If your instinct tells you something is going to be a waste of time and a source of unhappiness for you, it probably will. Follow your gut and refuse to take on the task, job, or responsibility. Your decision will be right nine times out of 10. And the one time you're wrong, you can usually reconsider and change your mind. Few decisions are permanent and irreversible.

Eliminate useless, time-consuming activities

My colleague, consultant Jeffrey Lant, has a full-time housekeeper. When I first learned this, I thought, "He's crazy—why should an able-bodied man have a housekeeper?" Now, I've come around to his point of view. The more hours you spend doing trivial activities, the fewer hours you have for important work.

Part of being a productive worker is avoiding interruptions and putting in the necessary hours. You can't do that effectively if you are dividing your time between too many things.

Because you have multiple responsibilities, the solution is to get other people to do as many of the noncritical activities as you are willing to give up or able to afford.

For instance, instead of dusting and vacuuming the house yourself, hire a cleaning service to do it for you. Instead of walking the dog in the morning, have your son or daughter do it while you're packing his or her lunch.

My approach is to off-load noncritical tasks, getting them off my list of responsibilities so I can concentrate on meaningful work. This strategy of "outsourcing"—asking or hiring others to do these "unimportant" tasks for you—is covered in detail in Chapter 6.

With an average life span of 75 years, we have only 27,375 days from the time we are born until the time we die. And because we're asleep for a third of that time, we have only 18,250 days we're actually awake and active.

How you spend this finite amount of time is mostly up to you. To maximize your productivity, income, and output, meaningful work must be a priority.

Value your time. "Time is the most precious currency of life, and how we spend it reflects what we truly value," writes Richard J. Leider in his book *The Power of Purpose* (Berrett-Koehler). "Once we have spent it, it is gone forever. It cannot be earned again."

If you prefer to nap, watch TV, or play cards, that's perfectly fine; but don't complain that your colleague, who spends those hours in front of the PC, is getting more work done than you are. It's your choice.

If you want it, ask for it

In the college cafeteria in my freshman year, the grill had a big sign posted on it that read: "Only one cheeseburger at a time—no double cheeseburgers." Ed, my friend standing in line in front of me, stepped up to the grill cook and ordered a double cheeseburger. Without a word, the cook flipped two burgers onto a bun and handed the burger to Ed. "How did you get him to do that?" I asked in wonder. Ed replied: "I asked."

This principle—if you want it, ask for it—is true in virtually ever facet of life—marriage, childhood, parenting, dating, real estate, consumer issues...and time management:

🕐 If you need more time on a project, ask. You just might get it.

🕐 If you don't want to take on an activity, tell the other person you don't want to do it. That person just might find someone else or do it him- or herself.

🕐 If a deadline, working arrangement, or situation is not right for you, tell the other person what you need to be comfortable with it. That person often adjusts his or her methods to fit your preferences.

🕐 Need a break? Ask for one. You'll get it more often than not.

The point is that if you ask, you often will get. If you don't ask, you will never get.

> Ask for what you want. Demand what you want. Insist on what you want. Not every time. Not in every situation. But more frequently than you do now.

Act as if you have only one life to live

If you don't have a sense of the finite quality of time, you have no real reason to off-load irrelevant tasks and stick to priorities. In my youth, I felt no urgency in life. After all, I reasoned, I would live forever...or about that long. There was always tomorrow: more days, more time. So I let others dictate the activities that filled my weeks.

But as Barbara Sher observes in her book *It's Only Too Late If You Don't Start Now* (Delacorte Press), all of that changes when you hit 40. You realize that you are mortal, time is racing by, and more than half your life is over. You have maybe 30 or 40 more years to live, maybe 10 to 20 or so years to achieve whatever professional goals you set for yourself. That's pretty short. You're no longer the *wunderkind*. If you want to make a dream come true, you have to start now.

So you become selfish about your time. You concentrate more on what's good for you, less on what everybody else demands. You start, probably for the first time, to see the deadline that is the end of your life.

If you can adapt this over-40 mind-set...even if you're under 40...you can gain tremendous leverage in negotiating the use of your time with others. For some, the over-40 mentality is sparked by the realization that there is a limited life span and that fact impels them to be more "me-oriented." For others, the over-40 mentality grows from having gained a measure of financial security. They become more in control and call their own shots more.

Whatever the source, the over-40 mind-set helps you realize that you do not have to please other people all the time. Doing this just takes too much of your time away from the things that please *you*. It took me an inordinate amount of time to learn to make my own time a priority. I had to learn to say no to requests, invitations, and offers that would neither make me happy nor help me achieve my goals. But once I did it, I found it was a liberating experience that gets easier with repetition.

Cut back on business travel

Even if you enjoy business travel, too many business trips steal precious time away from your priorities. In her book *SuccessAbilities* (JIST Works), Paula Ancona's suggests the following for cutting travel down to a reasonable level:

- Use phone calls, faxes, teleconferences, or videoconferences more often instead of traveling. Many businesses have cut their travel budgets this way.
- If your family life is a priority, have a family meeting to discuss how much travel is acceptable. Discuss the results with your supervisor.
- Explore with your boss ways to rearrange your schedule or duties so you can travel less.
- To avoid traveling on weekends, schedule meetings only on Tuesdays, Wednesdays, and Thursdays; or late in the day Monday or early Friday.

🕐 Tell your boss in advance when you can't travel (anniversaries, birthdays, special school functions).

🕐 When you travel, call home daily so you can stay involved. Parents of young children might call at bedtime to read a story over the phone.

🕐 When you're away, take an hour each day just for yourself. Relax or do something fun so you won't feel as if you are working around the clock when you travel.

🕐 Bring family members along once in a while. Turning some trips into mini-vacations is a way to build more family time into your schedule. According to an article in *American Demographics* (January, 1999), 24.4 million business trips included a child in 1997, compared to 7.4 million in 1987. "It appears that more Americans are turning their business trips into partial family vacations," says William Norman, president, Travel Industry Association of America.

For local travel, keep directions to each location stored in your portable appointment book, recommends direct marketer David Yale. That way, you always have the directions with you when heading to the appointment. It also eliminates the need to call people and ask them to re-fax directions they have already sent.

Review your to-do lists

Whatever else you do after reading this book, please don't neglect the simplest and most powerful personal productivity tool: your to-do lists (see Chapter 1 for a discussion of these lists). Writing in *Business News* (December 21, 1998), consultant Jeffrey Gittomer observes: "The basic underlying principle of time management is to do what's important first. The time management industry has made this principle far too complicated."

Jot down a list of priorities and stick to them. List the things you have to do in priority order, then do them in that priority. It really isn't much more complicated than that.

If you find yourself doing all kinds of tasks for other people that are not on your list, pull out your job description to remind yourself what you were originally hired to do. You might be surprised to find that you've taken on more duties than you're expected to perform. It's time to off-load.

> If you have some time on your hands, read several other books on time management (a few are listed in the Appendix). You can pick up a lot of useful ideas from each book.

Rid the meaningless to achieve the meaningful

"The difficulty in life is choice," says my friend Dr. Andrew Linick, a successful entrepreneur. "The cost of a thing is the amount of life you must exchange for it."

More and more, we should off-load those activities that are not truly meaningful to us. Success, to me, is being able to do more of the things I want to do, and less of the things I don't want to do.

A slew of new service businesses are cropping up to service the national desire to off-load the trivial, meaningless, and unimportant. Streamline, a company in Westwood, Massachusetts, lets families call in, e-mail, or fax their chore lists. Streamline sends workers to the customer's home to do such chores as grocery shopping, meal preparation, dry cleaning, video rental pick-up and drop-off, film processing, recycling, and delivering charitable donations to drop-off areas. The company claims it can save customers more than three hours a week.

Another company, LandJet, sells the ultimate sport utility vehicles and mini-vans. They offer a fully equipped vehicle (with built-in desk, fax, cell phone, VCR, refrigerator, and port for your laptop) that serves as an "office on wheels." They are advertised as "mobile office space." With these vehicles, every minute of travel is productive (of course it helps to have someone do the driving while you're working with a spreadsheet!).

You can even off-load on a less formal level. For instance, do you have piles of change all over your dresser, but you don't put it in coin wrappers because it takes too much time? You don't want to hire someone to do this work because the hourly rate would probably exceed the amount of unused change recovered. Here's a better solution: Ask your kids to do it. The reward? For every dollar of change they wrap, they get to keep 25 cents.

My wife and I used a similar strategy to get our kids to clean up the toy room and get rid of toys: They can gather together toys they no longer use and sell them to a used toy store. They can then keep the money in their bank accounts or use it to get something they really want, like a game for Sony Playstation. Our toy room is still overstuffed with toys, but the cash incentive has made the room a little cleaner and more livable than it was.

Make sure the effort matches the objective

Look before you leap; think before you speak; plan before you act. These simple instructions can save you an enormous amount of time and help you get much better results. Yet many people simply don't bother with these basics.

Your activities—whether making sales calls, servicing an account, designing a component, writing code—should support your business objectives. Much of the effort being expended today, however, doesn't. So it's an utter waste of time.

People who build Web sites without a plan, a strategy, or objectives are a good example of this problem. Many put up the site, spend $20,000, and get no business benefit out of it. Sure, they might get a lot of hits, but without a reason to generate those hits or a plan for converting them into customers, all that busy effort is largely wasted.

Another example: A colleague of mine spent a week of his time taking Excel training. "But you don't use spreadsheets in your business," I commented. "True," he said, "but I want to analyze my income and a computerized spreadsheet can help." This still made absolutely no sense to me. "Couldn't your book-keeper do this for you in a couple of hours?" I asked. My friend hadn't thought of that. It turned out that the bookkeeper did all the work in three hours for a total charge of $75—my friend never turned on a spreadsheet again. What a waste of training time!

Balance between success and contentment

My wife read this entire book in manuscript form. Her overall response: "You're nuts!" Although I've packed the book with nuggets I hope have value to you, she may be right: I'm obsessive about getting more done in less time. You may be similarly obsessed. Or you may not.

My advice: Take what works from this book. Adopt what's comfortable. Ignore the rest. Do you want to be the next Bill Gates? Are you a workaholic? Use these techniques to get more done every day and reach your goals faster.

Do you value leisure time? Are hobbies and vacations a passion with you? Do you want to spend more time with your spouse and children? Use the techniques in this book to get through your pile at work faster—so you have more time for yourself.

Be as productivity-conscious as I am. Or be more—or less. Whatever works best for you.

In an article in *Sun* magazine, John Taylor Gatto wrote:

> For five years I raced around digging ponds, chopping trees, clearing paths, pulling rocks, unclogging channels, planting—always making lists, plans, agendas. One day after finishing yet another important project, I made a list of all the things I had left to do. According to my schedule, I could begin enjoying my land 25 years down the line. Something was dreadfully wrong.

What John Gatto did after five years of frantic activity, you can do right now. So set your priorities. Work toward your goals. Achieve your dreams. Make yourself happy. You can do it! Your time is ultimately yours and yours alone. Make the most of it. Make every second count.

Appendix

Sources and Resources

Books

201 Ways to Manage Your Time Better by Alan Axelrod and Jim Holtje (McGraw-Hill, 1997)

500 Terrific Ideas for Organizing Everything by Sheree Bykofsky (Budget Book Service, 1997)

611 Ways to Do More in a Day by Stephanie Culp (Betterway Publications, 1998)

CyberMeeting by James L. Creighton and James W.R. Adams (American Management Association, 1997)

Getting Organized by Stephanie Winston (Warner Books, 1991)

No B.S. Time Management for Entrepreneurs by Dan Kennedy (Self Counsel Press, 1996)

The Complete Idiot's Guide to Managing Your Time by Jeff Davidson (Alpha Books, 1996)

The Management of Time by James T. McCay (Prentice Hall, 1959)

The 10 Natural Laws of Successful Time and Life Management by Hyrum W. Smith (Warner Books, 1995)

The Working Woman's Guide to Managing Time by Roberta Roesch and Alex MacKenzie (Prentice Hall, 1996)

Time Management for Dummies by Jeffrey J. Mayer (IDG Books, 1995)

Time Power by Charles R. Hobbs (Harper & Row, 1987)

Workaholics by Marilyn Machlowitz (New American Library, 1980)

Periodicals

The Organized Executive
GeorgeTown Publishing
1101 30th St., NW
Washington, DC
202-337-5980

Telecommuter's Digest
PO Box 86062
Gaithersburg, MD 20886-6062
301-963-0370

Organizations

National Association of Professional Organizers
1033 La Posada Suite 220
Austin, Texas 78752
512-206-0161
www.napo.net

Software

Act
Symantec
10201 Torre Avenue
Cupertino, CA 95014
800-441-7234

FastTrack
Fastech and Gelco Information Network
401 Parkway Dr.
Broomall, PA 19008
610-359-9200

GoldMine
GoldMine Software
17383 Sunset Blvd.
Ste. 301
Pacific Palisades, CA 90272
800-654-3526

InfoSelect
Micro Logic Corp.
PO Box 70
Hackensack, NJ 07602
201-342-6518

Multiactive Software
1090 West Pender St.
9th Floor
Vancouver, BC V6E2N7
800-804-6299

Pro-Mail
Software Marketing Associates
2080 Silas Deane Highway
Rocky Hill, CT 06067-2341
860-721-8929

Telemagic
17950 Preston Rd.
Ste. 800
Dallas, TX 75252
800-835-6244

Planning systems

Day Timers Inc.
One Day-Timer Plaza
Allentown, PA 18195-1551
800-225-5005

Web sites

Actioneer, Inc.
www.actioneer.com

Breathing Space Resource Center
www.breathingspace.com

The Productivity Institute
www.world-wide.com/productivity/

About the Author

Robert W. Bly is director of The Center for Technical Communication (CTC), a consulting firm providing on-site seminars in business communications, interpersonal skills, and personal productivity for corporate clients.

CTC has served more than 100 clients including AT&T, Lucent Technologies, Associated Global Systems, CoreStates, The Conference Board, BOC Gases, Wallace & Tiernan, Leviton Manufacturing, EBI Medical Systems, Optical Data Corporation, Value Rent-a-Car, Fielder's Choice, Grumman, Sony Corporation, Reed Travel Group, PSE&G, ADP, Agora Publishing, Medical Economics, Norwest Mortgage, and Ascom Timeplex.

Bob is the author of more than 40 books including *The Six-Figure Consultant* (Dearborn), *Selling Your Services* (Henry Holt & Co.), and *The Lead Generation Handbook* (Amacom).

Bob's articles have appeared in such publications as *Cosmopolitan, Writer's Digest, Business Marketing, Computer Decisions, Chemical Engineering, Science Books & Films, Direct Marketing, New Jersey Monthly*, and *Amtrak Express*. He is editor of the magazine *Bits & Pieces for Salespeople*, published monthly by Economics Press.

Bob holds a B.S. in chemical engineering from the University of Rochester. He has taught business communication at New

York University and held marketing positions with Koch Engineering and Westinghouse Electric Corporation. He is a member of the American Institute of Chemical Engineers, the Business Marketing Association, and the Institute of Management Consultants.

Questions and comments on *101 Ways to Make Every Second Count* can be sent to:

Bob Bly
Center for Technical Communication
22 E. Quackenbush Ave.
Dumont, NJ 07628
Phone: 201-385-1220
Fax: 201-385-1138
E-mail: rwbly@bly.com
Web: www.bly.com

Index